Kaylee's Choice

Kaylee's Choice

Kaylee O'Shay, Irish Dancer

Rod Vick

Laikituk Creek Publishing

Kaylee's Choice
Kaylee O'Shay, Irish Dancer

Laikituk Creek Publishing
Mukwonago, Wisconsin

Manufactured in the United States of America

ISBN: 978-0-6923173-8-9

For Haley Marie

Foreword

Rod Vick

The world of Irish dance is about more than just pretty costumes and shiny tiaras. In fact, if that's what you're thinking, maybe you should put down this book and back slowly away.

While the costumes are amazing, Irish dance is far more than glitter. It's about a breathtaking and sometimes mysterious culture. It's sweat and repetition and sore muscles. It's standing rigidly in front of hundreds, even thousands of people, knowing that months of sacrifice and practice have all added up to what will happen in the next ninety seconds. It's speed and strength and grace and athleticism.

It's passion and friendship and love.

It's about dreaming. Not just any kind of dreaming. It's about dreaming *big* dreams.

This is the world my family discovered when my daughter began her career as an Irish dancer, a world that she embraced lovingly and which changed our whole family in ways we could scarcely have imagined. The stories of Kaylee O'Shay are not my daughter's stories, but they were inspired by the challenges and journeys faced by all dancers as they grow older and become more passionately connected to the world of Irish dance. Kaylee, the ten-year-old main character in this book, hopes dance will one day take her to Ireland and the World Championships.

I hope you enjoy following Kaylee's journey. And I wish you the best of luck in following your own passion. But know that, whether in this book or in real life, it won't be a tame ride!

Sincerely,

Rod Vick
Author of the Kaylee O'Shay, Irish Dancer series

Two roads diverged in a wood, and I -
I took the one less traveled by

– Robert Frost

One

Some parents pinched themselves, certain they were dreaming. Others, amazed at the speed and grace of the girl on the soccer pitch, found themselves thinking "college scholarship" or "World Cup" or just "wow!" Then they shook their heads, remembering that she was merely ten years old. Many simply stood along the sidelines, mouths agape like cave dwellers seeing a fighter jet for the first time.

Kaylee O'Shay fielded the pass from Heather and darted up the right side, an emerald blur in her Green Storm jersey. Nearing the goal, she faked to the left. The crowd *oohed*—even parents from the other team. Then Kaylee slashed right (*Ah!* went the crowd) leaving the Orange Wave defender so off-balance that the poor girl actually tripped on her own spikes and executed a textbook butt-landing.

The smallest girl on her team, a graceless fusion of freckles, dirty blonde curls and skinny legs—yet here Kaylee was, making it look easy, poised to score the goal that would give her team the fall league championship. Despite her breakneck speed, she noticed the stunned looks on the faces of parents along the sidelines, faces that seemed to say, *That's our Kaylee! She's amazing!*

With only one Wave player to beat, Kaylee cut toward the goal and effortlessly dished the ball off to Green Storm teammate Brittany Hall. The defender adjusted, but Brittany tapped a side-foot pass brilliantly back to Kaylee, who sent a rocket into the far corner of the net.

She just had time to glance at the sidelines where Michael Black—the cutest boy in the fifth grade—stood among the spectators and winked to acknowledge her triumph. Then her Green Storm teammates surrounded her, patting her on the back, chanting *Kaylee! Kaylee!*

"Kaylee!"

Heather's voice roused her from the daydream.

"Kaylee! Wake up! She's right on top of you!"

Kaylee O'Shay blinked the last of the dream world away. The Wave player with the ball loomed just a few feet in front of her. She stuck out a foot awkwardly to try and steal it, but the other girl cut left, and in a blink, Kaylee found herself two steps behind.

Fortunately, Brittany blocked the Wave player's path and deftly plucked the ball away. Two players in orange converged immediately, and Brittany lofted a pass toward Kaylee.

"Go, Kaylee!" cried Heather. "Open field to the goal!"

Kaylee's heart beat faster as she realized that the Wave defenders had drifted away in pursuit of the ball. Because Kaylee had been so slow in reacting, she stood alone and could now take it all the way up the right side. She gave it a tap, began to pick up speed . . . and tripped over the ball. She hit the turf hard, losing her wind and getting a mouthful of grass. Out of the corner of her eye, she saw the ball squirt away.

Her teammates groaned.

I hate this game, thought Kaylee, watching helplessly as an orange-clad girl took the ball in the opposite direction.

Kaylee pulled herself into a standing position, but before she began her pursuit, three whistle blasts signaled the end of the game. Orange Wave players squealed, traded hugs and high fives.

The Green Storm lined up glumly, trotted through the ritual hand-slap with the winning team, and headed over to where their coach stood waiting.

Heather Chandler walked with Brittany a few feet in front of Kaylee, speaking in the kind of fierce whisper that you want someone else to hear. "We should have won that game. The goal was wide open, but *O'Shrimp* blew it again."

"A four-year-old could have made that shot," said Heather. "Too bad O'Shrimp isn't as tall as most four-year-olds, or she might have had a chance."

Kaylee's cheeks burned and tears welled in her eyes.

"Good game, Storm!" called the coach as they reached the sideline. "You never quit! Great effort! I'm proud of you all!"

Some of the girls looked at their feet. Others focused on some point in the distance. No one made eye contact with the coach.

"Amanda, good hustle!" said Coach. "Heather, nice goal in the first half! Stephanie, you made some awesome stops out there!" He had something positive to offer every player—another ritual they endured after each game. "You really worked hard today!" said the coach when he came to Kaylee.

She heard a snicker and then Brittany's voice, this time low enough so that the coach could not hear. "Worked hard to help the *other* team win."

Kaylee turned abruptly and walked back across the field.

"Kaylee?" called her coach, but she did not stop. The field had cleared, although a handful of parents waited on the far side, collapsible chairs stuffed into colorful nylon sleeves slung over their shoulders. She walked past all of them to the parking lot where she sat in the grass in front of her family's car.

Now the tears gushed forth.

At one time, soccer had been different. When Kaylee was six, it had been about running after the ball and laughing with the other girls on the team and brightly-colored uniforms. And treats after games. But even then, soccer had been her father's idea. He had been a pretty decent player in high school and college, and though he had never actually said so, she knew that he wanted to see his little girl follow in his footsteps. Unfortunately, as Kaylee grew older, she never showed much of a gift for the game. Still, she had played for her father. She had played even though it had begun to hurt.

It hurt to be the worst player on the team.

And the shortest.

It hurt to be made fun of by her teammates week after week.

It hurt to be the one who always had trouble learning the new skills in practice.

It hurt when they blamed her for . . . everything.

She looked back toward the field and saw Brittany slowly approaching the parking lot. Michael Black walked beside her, listening to the recap of Brittany's personal highlights no doubt. Or her assessment of her teammates' inferior play. Blonde and cute, Brittany had already begun to attract the attention of ten- and eleven-year-old boys whose brains had been zonked by the Hormone Fairy's wand. (Kaylee felt that this was mostly because Brittany was a little "chunky", and this made her seem a bit rounder in the places where a ten- or eleven-year-old boy might notice roundness.) The two passed without noticing her, a bit of good fortune for which Kaylee was especially thankful.

I wish he'd hurry up, thought Kaylee, wiping her eyes with the sleeve of her jersey.

As she lowered her arm, she saw that the coach was now kneeling beside her, his eyes sad and sympathetic. "Kaylee, I'm sorry if I said something that upset you."

Kaylee pushed herself to her feet. "Don't worry about it," she said abruptly, taking a step toward the car behind her. "Let's just go home, Dad."

Two

When her team lost a soccer game on a Saturday morning, Kaylee always hoped that something good would occur later in the day to even things out.

Later on this September Saturday, her grandmother set the house on fire.

Not much damage thankfully, but Kaylee wondered what might have happened if she and her father had not arrived home from the soccer game when they did. Grandma Birdsall had placed a microwaveable dinner into the toaster oven, which, Mr. O'Shay pointed out, was clearly forbidden by the fine print on the box. By the time Kaylee and her father walked in, black smoke billowed out as if someone had decided to cook a tire. Her father frantically slipped on kitchen mitts and carried the toaster oven into the driveway. Tom O'Shay, a slim man with thinning brown hair and gentle, hazel eyes, returned coughing and red-faced, muttering unpleasantly while he switched on the kitchen fan and opened all the windows in the house.

"This is just great!" Kaylee heard him mutter, though he also muttered a few things that she had been warned to never even *think*. "Last month the washing machine breaks down! Now we'll probably have to repaint the kitchen! This is just great!"

When he wasn't coaching soccer, Tom O'Shay worked as an associate manager at the hardware store in Rosemary, Wisconsin. Being an associate manager meant that he got to wear a special pin on his yellow Rosemary Hardware shirt, but the pay really wasn't much better than if he had been a part-timer. As a result, he counted the pennies at the O'Shay household carefully. And if something needed to be replaced or repaired, he often said things like: "This is just great!" And some worse things as well.

As Mr. O'Shay stood in the kitchen, apparently trying to decide whether to say the worst things of all or to simply begin scrubbing the blackened wall, Kaylee's nine-year-old brother, Will, padded down the stairs from his room, an open box of breakfast cereal under his arm. "What stinks?"

This helped Kaylee's father decide, and he launched into a treasure trove of observations, most focusing on how the whole house could have gone up in flames because Will had been too wrapped up in his "mind-numbing video games!"

With her father upset, her grandmother in tears, her brother clueless and the house smelling like burned plastic with beef gravy, Kaylee quietly slipped into the garage, found her helmet and pedaled off down Cranberry Street on her bike. Gliding beneath burr oaks and silver maples whose leaves were just beginning to hint at the gorgeous shades of gold and scarlet to come, Kaylee began to feel better. Saturdays were supposed to be fun, thought Kaylee, and most of the time they were. It just so happened that on this particular Saturday she had single-handedly lost the game for her soccer team and her house had nearly burned down. And Brittany had been Brittany.

Now, however, sunlight hit her like sprays of golden paint as she coasted past the small, neat houses in the older neighborhood, heading toward downtown Rosemary and then on to Jackie's house. She felt her spirits stir, rustle their delicate wings and prepare to take flight.

That was when her front tire went flat.

Home was eight blocks away. On the other hand, just around the next corner was a gas station where she could put air in the tire and hope it wouldn't leak out until she arrived at Jackie's house. Kaylee leaned the bicycle against her hip and slipped her hands into her pockets. Empty. The automated pump at the gas station cost a quarter for two minutes of compressed air.

With a sigh, she headed toward the Stitchin' Kitchen. She had wanted to bypass the shop, go directly to Jackie's, but now it seemed she had no choice—unless she wanted to push the bike with its mushy tire the whole distance.

It took just a few minutes for Kaylee to reach the older building on a downtown side street. She leaned her bike near the door and entered, a tiny brass bell above the door announcing her arrival.

"Kaylee!" said her mother, looking up from the small stack of paperwork spread before her on the countertop. Kaylee glanced around the shop. An older woman examining fabric bolts near the back of the store appeared to be the only customer.

Kaylee's mother, Beth, a short woman with a pretty, freckled face and wavy-brown hair cut in a typical, prim mom-do, owned the Stitchin' Kitchen, a combination fabric store and coffee shop. Her mother had been an elementary school teacher when Kaylee was younger, but a year and a half ago, she had decided to follow a longtime dream and open her own business. "Lots of women like to sew," she had explained to the family. "And they like good coffee, too. Here they can have both."

Old women like to sew, Kaylee had thought at the time, remembering the three sewing machines in her grandmother's room. And ever since she had taken a sip from her father's cup, she had wondered why people made such a big deal about coffee. "It's bitter and it's got no fizz," she had complained. "I'll take an orange soda any day!"

Despite her daughter's advice, Beth O'Shay had rented space in a former antique shop in downtown Rosemary, a place with large display windows out front and a worn hardwood floor. She had brought in secondhand shelves and display racks, constructed a charming coffee bar near one of the front windows, and surrounded it with half a dozen sewing stations on which people might rent time. On these same machines, Beth O'Shay also taught lessons throughout the day. Her clients sewed and sipped happily. Unfortunately, the cash required to pay the rent and to keep the shelves well-stocked with the latest fabrics and patterns and coffee flavors had left the Stitchin' Kitchen squeaking by most months, and not quite able to squeak on others.

Based on recent conversations, this month was apparently a mouse with serious laryngitis.

"How'd the game go?" said Mrs. O'Shay, stepping out from behind the coffee bar and kissing her daughter on the forehead. "You smell smoky. Is your dad burning leaves?"

Kaylee did not want to talk about the game. She did not want to talk about anything. However, since she was here, she knew she would have to tell her mother everything. She couldn't just forget to mention something like Grandma almost burning down the house, especially after her mother's "burning leaves" question.

Beth O'Shay's face darkened and she bit her lip as she listened to the details. "Oh, Mom," she whispered as Kaylee finished.

Grandma Birdsall, age 70, had lived in the spare bedroom for almost a year and a half. Beth O'Shay had suggested the arrangement after her mother, twice married and now twice widowed (Grandpa Birdsall had passed away five years earlier), complained that her own house had just gotten "too big for one person to handle".

"Grandma wasn't hurt at all, was she?" asked Mrs. O'Shay, the fingers on her left hand starting a nervous roll on the countertop.

Kaylee shook her head.

Her mother's face grew wary. "Did your father say anything?"

"'This is just great!'" reported Kaylee.

Mrs. O'Shay nodded grimly.

Having delivered the news, Kaylee was about to leave when she remembered her real reason for coming. Her mother found a couple of quarters in her pocket, gave her daughter a hug, added the usual cautions about bicycle safety and finished by telling Kaylee to be home by four o'clock. Kaylee backtracked to the gas station and used one quarter to fill the tire, saving the other in case it leaked on the way back. Then she resumed her trip to Jackie's.

Jackie Kizobu had joined the Green Storm soccer team two years earlier and had quickly become Kaylee's best friend. Kaylee liked to think of her as the "anti-Brittany": Jackie was Japanese, a twig with braces so elaborate that they probably could pick up radio signals from distant galaxies; Brittany was a blonde rock pile with teeth so white and perfect it hurt to look at them. Jackie was one of the worst soccer players on the Green Storm—an honor she shared with Kaylee; Brittany was the best girl athlete in the fifth grade. Jackie was nice; Brittany was . . . the best girl athlete in the fifth grade.

After saying hello to Mrs. Kizobu, the two girls disappeared into Jackie's room, which Kaylee observed was easily as messy as her own.

"I can't play soccer worth worms, my grandmother is going to kill us all, and we never have any money," she told her friend while settling onto the explosion of books and t-shirts and underwear that passed for Jackie's bedroom floor. "I wish my mom had never quit her teaching job!"

Jackie pushed a button to start her CD player. "If we were professional soccer players, like Angelo Zizzo, we'd never have to worry about money." She raised her eyes to one of the seven Angelo Zizzo posters tacked onto the walls of her room.

Kaylee sighed, finding a pink sock with her free hand, flipping it back and forth. "I know my grandmother's got some money in the bank. At least that's what my dad says. He thinks she should pay more for food and groceries and stuff. Mom says she's our guest, she's family. Dad says if that's so, then she should be willing to help out when the family budget comes up short."

"What does your grandma say?" asked Jackie.

Although Kaylee had always known her grandmother to be generous with her affections, she had also gotten the impression that Grandma Birdsall was cautious when it came to money.

"I think she wants us to stand on our own two feet," said Kaylee.

They listened to music for awhile. Then Jackie seemed to remember something. "Hey, good game today!"

Kaylee grunted. "I kind of lost it for us."

"You did great!" said Jackie. "The Orange Wave is an awesome team and we almost beat them."

"I don't know," said Kaylee, sniffing the pink sock and then tossing it across the room. "Sometimes I think maybe soccer isn't right for me."

"Don't say things like that in front of Angelo!" said Jackie with exaggerated alarm. "You can't quit the Storm! What would *I* do? Start hanging out with Brittany and Heather?"

"I'm not going to quit," said Kaylee, laughing at the thought of Jackie, Brittany and Heather sharing girl talk. "I like some of the girls on the team. I like being coached by my dad. I just wish I could play better, you know? And grow a foot!"

"Have you looked at your parents?" asked Jackie as if reminding her friend that the sun rose in the east. "You don't have the genes for another foot! Unless you've got some long-lost uncles in the NBA."

Kaylee sighed. "Dad jokes about it. He says all the O'Shays had to stay short because Great-Great-

Grandpa O'Shay gambled away his fortune, and when he built the family's ancestral home in Ireland, he could only afford enough wood to make the ceiling five feet ten inches tall."

"Your family has an ancestral home?" Jackie sounded impressed.

"I think it's just a story my dad made up," said Kaylee. "It's better than telling everyone we've got pygmy genes." She thought about this for a moment. "Maybe not better, but funnier. At least to my dad it's funny. Grandma Birdsall's side is short, too."

"My dad is shorter than yours," noted her friend. "But my mom is a little taller."

"Yup," said Kaylee. "We're both doomed."

"We'll just have to work harder," said Jackie, now sounding like a cheerleader. "Hey, maybe we can go to soccer camp this summer!"

Kaylee looked at her watch. "I've got to go."

Jackie found a hand pump in her garage and the two girls re-inflated the bicycle tire, which was almost flat again. Then Kaylee headed back, spending her last quarter on more air at the downtown gas station.

How could her parents ever afford to send her to soccer camp? thought Kaylee sadly as she returned to Cranberry Street and its strikingly ordinary houses. They probably couldn't afford to replace the scorched toaster oven.

Coasting to a stop across the street from her house, she noticed how small and plain it looked. No brick or stone or elegant natural wood on the outside, just boring white siding. Her parents referred to it as a "Cape Cod-style" house. To Kaylee, this meant that if you were unlucky enough to get the upstairs bedroom—her cereal-addicted brother Will had actually ASKED for it—you bumped your head a lot on the slanted ceiling. If Great-Great-Grandfather O'Shay really had built an ancestral home, Will probably knew how it felt to have lived there.

Two years ago they had lived in a bigger house with a much larger yard and no old people who couldn't tell the difference between a microwave and a toaster oven. Now it seemed like everything was smaller and more crowded.

She didn't want to go inside. Her mother's old Chevy sat in the driveway behind the blackened remains of the toaster oven. Would her parents be arguing over Grandma Birdsall? Would they make Kaylee help wash the walls? Would her grandmother be crying? Would it still stink like burned plastic with beef gravy? For a moment she considered pedaling back to Jackie's house. However, as she moved the bicycle forward, she knew she could not do that.

Her tire had gone flat again.

Three

The teachers dropped big homework on them on Mondays, as if they thought the fifth graders had forgotten everything after being exposed to cartoons, play and parents for two days. Stretched across her bed, Kaylee needed to finish eight more math problems--but she couldn't concentrate. Instead, she flipped on the television set in her room.

"You'll never have a TV in your room," her mother had told her. "It'd be too much of a distraction."

Then they had moved into the smaller home and Grandma Birdsall had moved in with them. The TV in the living room made too much noise at night, and Grandma liked to go to bed early. It had been moved into the O'Shay parents' bedroom, which meant that whenever the whole family wanted to watch something, Kaylee's father lugged the TV to the living room, or they crowded on top of her parents' bed. While inconvenient, the arrangement offered fringe benefits for the O'Shay children: The old eighteen-inch TV from the pre-Grandma Birdsall period now sat in Kaylee's room. And since her room was so crowded, the TV from her grandmother's house rested in Will's upstairs bedroom, helping him to save, conquer or destroy the universe, depending on his choice of video game.

Although Kaylee liked having a TV, it made her more conscious of the small size of her bedroom. Her twin bed, tiny desk, crate-sized bureau and the modest TV took up most of the space along the deep green walls. The center of the room was usually carpeted with clothing, though whether it was soiled or simply clean clothing that had never been put away properly was anyone's guess.

Our whole house is too small, thought Kaylee. That wasn't going to change any time soon. The O'Shays had moved into the smaller, ranch-style home at about the same time Mrs. O'Shay had opened the Stitchin' Kitchen. The reason, according to Kaylee's father, was that they needed to "downsize", to trim expenses so that Beth O'Shay could afford the start-up costs of her new business. "Smaller house, smaller house payment," Mr. O'Shay had stated logically.

These memories, plus the memory of the unfinished homework, convinced Kaylee that she still lacked the necessary focus to return to her studies. She watched a comedy for a few minutes, walking to the kitchen for a drink of water during a commercial. When she returned, the TV announcer was urging viewers to pick up their phones right now and order tickets for *Isle of Green Fire* at Milwaukee's Historic Nicolet Theater. The price flashed on the screen.

That much for one ticket? thought Kaylee, aghast. *Nothing's worth that kind of money. Especially not some play about a fire at a toxic waste dump.*

But then she watched the teaser. It wasn't a play. At least nothing like she had seen before. It was dancers performing to driving yet playful Celtic music. They stood like pencils in their dark costumes, arms to their sides as if held by bolts. But their feet moved like pistons.

No.

Far more precise, complex and . . . and beautiful than pistons. But so incredibly fast!

There had to be some trick.

Yet, as she watched, she realized that there were no digital special effects. These were not robots. It was their own feet, and they were really moving that fast.

Maybe something is worth that kind of money, Kaylee thought.

Then a woman appeared on stage. Her jeweled costume caught the lights like fireworks, and her feet were easily as fast as the men. She took command of the theater, as dazzling as a champion gymnast, as beautiful as an Olympic figure skater, as powerful as a goddess. The announcer's voice returned. "See Elena McGinty in the only Milwaukee performance of *Isle of Green Fire* this year!"

I used to dance, thought Kaylee. She had taken beginning tap and ballet at Miss Suzie's for several years when she was younger. *I enjoyed it, too. It was fun.* The kind of dancing she had just seen on TV, that looked like fun, too. It also looked exciting.

Much more exciting than the math problems she still had to finish.   As the comedy resumed, Kaylee turned off the TV.

In school on Tuesday, Mrs. Mallory gave her students computer time to conduct Internet research on "westward expansion". Kaylee quickly printed a couple of articles on Lewis and Clark.   As she retrieved the pages from the printer, she noticed that her teacher appeared to be helping two boys on the far side of the room. From the exasperated look on Mrs. Mallory's face, Kaylee determined that she would be busy for awhile. She returned to her seat and typed *Isle of Green Fire* into the browser. *Well,* she told herself, *if you travel west far enough, you eventually come to Ireland.*

Kaylee clicked onto a web site whose home page featured a magnificent photo of a woman in mid-leap.

Elena McGinty.

Her costume sparkled, her toes could chisel granite and she smiled as if it were the first day of summer vacation. The words *Elena McGinty's Isle of Green Fire* exploded across the top of the screen in a type face that actually resembled green flames. Buttons along the left side advertised links to

TICKETS, PERFORMANCE SCHEDULE, PHOTO SAMPLER, CAST BIOGRAPHIES and ISLE OF GREEN FIRE: THE STORY. Kaylee clicked on the last of these, bringing up another photo of Elena McGinty in a different yet equally striking costume. Underneath was an explanation:

Elena McGinty's Isle of Green Fire is an Irish-American Masterpiece!

Born in Ireland, Ms. McGinty started dancing at the age of four, winning a World Championship title at sixteen. Three years later, after many additional honors, Ms. McGinty was invited to audition for a major touring company in the United States. Within two years, she became the lead female dancer, thrilling audiences and earning raves from reviewers.

At twenty-four, Ms. McGinty formed her own company and developed *Isle of Green Fire,* a breathtaking re-telling of Ireland's historic struggle for social justice—brought to the stage in dance! Ms. McGinty, who is honored to have danced the lead in every performance of *Isle of Green Fire*, electrifies audiences everywhere she goes with dance movements that seem to defy gravity and dare the human eye to keep up!

After finishing her homework that night, Kaylee approached her mother, who she found poring over a stack of receipts and invoices scattered atop the kitchen table.

"Could I take dance lessons?"

Her mother actually smiled.

"You used to take dance lessons a few years ago at Miss Suzie's Studio."

It seemed almost every little girl in Rosemary took lessons at Miss Suzie's, starting at about age four or five. The majority lost interest by the time they were nine or ten, though Miss Suzie coached about two dozen teen girls who made up a traveling performance group.

"You picked up steps fast, even when you were just five," Kaylee's mother recalled proudly. "Sometimes the other little girls looked like they didn't have a clue, but you were always right on the beat."

Kaylee smiled at the memory. "I want to dance again."

Her mother nodded. "I can give Miss Suzie a call tomorrow—"

"Not at Miss Suzie's," interrupted Kaylee. When she realized how abrupt she sounded, she offered an explanation. "There's nothing wrong with Miss Suzie's Studio. It was great. I had fun. But I want to try something different."

Beth O'Shay's eyes narrowed slightly. "Different?"

"I want to try Irish dance!" She explained what she had seen on TV and during her Internet research. Her mother at first seemed completely shocked by this request, as if her daughter had asked to become a Hollywood stunt person. Then she listened warily.

"I suppose it won't hurt to check around." It seemed to Kaylee that her mother said this as if she were in a dream. "I'll do it sometime this week when things get slow at the Stitchin' Kitchen."

Four

The ball rolled in front of the goal where Brittany, charging hard, booted it so that it took off like a bullet.

Right into the net.

"Nice," said Kaylee's father, clapping his hands. "Next!"

Now Heather sprinted toward a spot about fifteen meters in front of the goal. Coach O'Shay rolled another soccer ball, and Heather sent this one into the left corner of the net. Several of her teammates clapped or shouted encouragement.

Kaylee waited in line behind Jackie and Naomi. Both put it in, though Jackie hit hers poorly and it barely crossed the line.

"Go!" shouted Coach O'Shay as he rolled another ball. Kaylee raced to meet it. She hit it solidly--so solidly that even she could hardly believe it. Unfortunately, it slammed into the top bar above the goal and bounced back toward her. A few of her teammates chuckled.

"Nice," said Brittany, though her tone of voice and the smirk on her face suggested that she meant just the opposite.

"Good try, Kaylee!" shouted Jackie, whose compliment sounded much more sincere.

"Good, strong shot!" called Kaylee's father.

Kaylee sighed and jogged to the end of the line. That seemed to be the story of her life these days. She tried hard, but couldn't quite put it into the net.

Later they dribbled around cones, ran sprints, played a modified version of keep away and finally broke for water.

"You're really hustling out there today, Kaylee," said her father, coming over to kneel next to her as she drank from her water bottle.

This was one of those moments when she loved soccer. When she was completely honest with herself, she had to admit that she enjoyed the competition, the speed, the footwork. But the harassment from jerks like Brittany and Heather made her feel angry and helpless. Another problem was coming to practice every week knowing that she was one of the weaker players, and knowing that everyone else on the team knew it, too. Of course, she could have easily dealt with Problem One (harassment) and Problem Two (lack of talent) if not for Problem Three, which was that she just didn't have her father's passion for the game.

"Thanks, Dad."

"You've got a good, strong leg, sweetheart," he added, patting her forearm. "You're a butterfly waiting to break out of the cocoon."

She felt more like the caterpillar during the second half of practice. Most of the half was spent scrimmaging, and it seemed to Kaylee that she was always just a step slower than her teammates, a step behind wherever it was that she was supposed to be.

She sat quietly on the way home. Eventually her father asked what was the matter.

Kaylee shook her head and repeated the sentiment that she had shared on the phone with Jackie. "I just don't know whether I'm cut out for soccer. Everyone is better than I am."

"That's not true," said Mr. O'Shay. "You're very steady. Very dependable."

Kaylee let out a noisy breath. "Steady and dependable aren't the same as being good. I feel like I'm letting everyone down."

"Kaylee," said her father, "you're making steady progress. I've got us signed up for an indoor league starting this winter. I'll be coaching. Most of the girls you already play with will be on the team. It will really polish your skills!" He beamed at her in glances, while also keeping his eyes on the road. Kaylee suddenly felt like the caterpillar again—a caterpillar trying to creep across a freeway during rush hour.

Indoor league. Now Brittany and Heather could make fun of her year-round.

On the other hand, Jackie was nice. And Kaylee enjoyed being coached by her father. He had bought her a tiny soccer ball when she was only two. She hadn't been able to really kick it. Just sort of bumped into it and watched it roll away. Half of her toddler clothes were tiny soccer jerseys. He had taken her to her first professional soccer match in Milwaukee when she was four. Kaylee could not think of a time when her father hadn't been there for her.

She smiled at him. "Indoor league. Sounds great, Dad."

Her father reached over and tousled her hair with his right hand. "Say, maybe you and I can do something together later on," he said.

Kaylee smiled up at him. "I'd like that!"

"Great!" said her father. "Put on some old clothes when we get home. Something that won't matter if you get it dirty."

Were they going hiking? Borrowing paintball guns from a neighbor? Maybe working on the tree house that her father had started but never quite finished. "What are we going to do?" she asked.

"Today's the day we repaint the kitchen!" said Mr. O'Shay brightly. "Won't that be fun?"

Five

When Kaylee arrived home from school on Thursday, her mother met her with a concerned look. She sat with Kaylee on the living room couch.

"I called around," Mrs. O'Shay said, and then gave a sigh. "It's a lot different from Miss Suzie's, you know."

Kaylee's stomach felt the way it did when she was seven and her mother informed her that Domino, her pet Guinea pig had died. "What do you mean?"

"At Miss Suzie's studio, you learned tap and ballet," said Mrs. O'Shay. "If you would have stayed in her group, you would have learned jazz, too. At Irish dance schools, you only learn Irish dances." She gave another sigh. "The lessons are very expensive."

Kaylee felt her mouth go dry. She knew that anything which might be described as "expensive" was not a particularly welcome topic of discussion in their household.

"They can't be that much more expensive," said Kaylee.

Her mother's raised eyebrows were sufficient response.

"Then there's the special shoes," said Mrs. O'Shay. "You would need a kind of soft shoe called ghillies." The way she pronounced it made Kaylee think of something a small fish would breathe through.

"I needed special shoes at Suzie's, too," noted Kaylee.

"Those were ballet shoes," said her mother. "Ghillies are about three times as expensive."

"Then," countered Kaylee, "I'll take really good care of them so they last three times as long."

Her mother gave a tired smile. "That's just the start. You'll eventually need a pair of hard shoes. If you stick with it."

"Like taps?" asked Kaylee. "I suppose they're three times as expensive, too."

Her mother chuckled. "If only. We could buy a new television set with the same money."

Kaylee felt like crying. "Well, we've already got three TVs."

Beth O'Shay did not want to continue, but it was unavoidable. "There's the costume."

Folding her arms across her chest, Kaylee asked, "Are they as expensive as new TVs, too?"

Her mother smiled wryly. "60-inch, wide screen, flat panel."

Kaylee's eyes widened. "How can anybody afford to do this kind of dancing?"

"I don't know," said her mother. "All I know is that we can't."

"But Mom!" cried Kaylee, standing.

"Honey," said her mother, her eyes set to the pleading channel, "it's a lot of money. And right now, we just can't afford it."

Kaylee ran toward her room, thinking, *We'll never be able to afford it.*

She passed her grandmother's room on the way. *Dad's right!* Kaylee thought bitterly. *She lives here for almost nothing. If we started charging her rent, we'd be able to afford lots of things.*

Of course Kaylee knew her mother wouldn't hear of it. "She's family," Mrs. O'Shay had often said. "Should I start charging Kaylee and Will, too? Maybe you've forgotten all the help my mother has given us over the years."

Kaylee remembered that they had lived in Grandma Birdsall's home for three months after they had sold their former house, but before they had been able to move into their current residence on Cranberry Street. She also knew that her parents always received a check from Grandma at Christmas. The amount remained a secret, but it never failed to make her mother cry or cause her father to give Grandma a big hug.

"Kaylee?"

Her grandmother's voice. Kaylee didn't want her grandmother to see the tears, and so she quickly wiped her eyes on the sleeves of her hooded pink fleece pullover.

Grandma Birdsall came to the door, a concerned look on her face. "Is everything all right?"

Kaylee wanted to say, *Everything except you started the kitchen on fire and I had to help repaint it.* Of course, she didn't.

"Yes," said Kaylee, standing at an angle to her grandmother, reluctant to make eye contact. "No." A pause. "It's nothing."

"I hate to see you sad," said Grandma Birdsall. Then another thought seemed to strike her. "Could you help me with something?" She motioned into her bedroom.

Kaylee sighed. It was getting late. She still had homework to finish. Her dreams were in the toilet. Now, her grandmother wanted to leech away more of her valuable time.

"Fine," said Kaylee, defeated, following the old woman into through the doorway.

Grandma Birdsall's room was packed with the remains of her life. A day bed rested against the west wall. Even without a full-size bed in the room, there was little space to walk. A hand-tied rag rug partially covered the wooden floor. Here and there, several large woven baskets sat like pudgy visitors, bulging with yarn or books or antique walking sticks or other items that most people would find uninteresting. Corrugated boxes were stacked along half of the east wall. The other half contained the closet door, and a space between the closet and boxes where a sewing machine rested on a narrow table. A large window took up most of the south wall, although there stood yet another sewing machine that partially blocked this. The north wall where they entered was home to a dresser--upon which dozens of photographs, both framed and unframed, were situated—and a wide shelf containing plastic boxes, rolls of fabric, and threads wrapped onto large cones. Most of the light-blue wall space visible above these items held shelves, upon which Grandma's collections of knick-knacks rested. A faint lilac odor hung in the air.

"There's a box on the upper shelf of my closet," said her grandmother, opening the door for Kaylee. "I'm afraid I'll hurt myself if I try to get it. Do you think you could manage?"

Kaylee muttered a "sure" and easily brought the wide box onto the middle of the day bed as her grandmother directed. They sat, Kaylee on one side of the box, her grandmother on the other. Grandma Birdsall lifted the top flaps, peered over the edge, stuck in a hand to move some things around and finally brought out several scraps of material.

"I used to make full-sized bed quilts," said Grandma Birdsall. "But I can't do that very easily anymore. My quilting frame wouldn't fit in this room, and I really can't ask your parents to let me set it up out in the living room. They've been more than generous already."

That's for sure, thought Kaylee.

"However," continued her grandmother, "I've been thinking of making some smaller quilts, the kind that could be used as wall hangings or lap quilts or car blankets. I could do that without the frame."

Kaylee stifled a yawn. *That's just great, grandma. Why are you telling all of this to me?*

"I thought maybe you could help me."

The suggestion caught Kaylee by surprise. "Me?"

Grandma Birdsall smiled. "I remember when you were seven or eight, we used to sew together all the time. We made puppets and embroidered dish towels and even a little skirt. I have to confess that I miss that. I wondered if maybe you would like me to teach you to make a quilt."

Kaylee did not say anything right away, but her eyes traveled to the material in the box.

"It would just be a small quilt," her grandmother said when it seemed to her the silence had gone just a bit too long. "And we could make it any design you like. I have magazines you could look through. Some of them are very cool."

Hearing her grandmother use the word cool almost forced a grimace from Kaylee. "I don't know if I'd be very good at quilting, grandma," she said slowly.

"Oh, don't worry about that," said Grandma Birdsall, her eyes shining. "I could teach you with no problem. From what I remember, you had a bit of a knack for sewing."

Again, Kaylee was silent. After a moment she brought her eyes from the box to her grandmother's face.

"Wouldn't you rather sew down at the Stitchin' Kitchen with all of the other ladies?" asked Kaylee hopefully.

Her grandmother smiled patiently. "I don't really know anyone there except your mother. And when I go there, it just feels . . . awkward. Like your mother is babysitting me." She looked lovingly at her granddaughter. "But my biggest reason is that I want to do this with you, honey," said the old woman, and Kaylee knew that she was trapped. Just great. As if my life wasn't decaying quickly enough. Now my free time is going to be spent playing Betsy Ross in the graveyard of rejected fabrics.

Kaylee forced a thin smile. "Sure."

Six

When Kaylee was in a bad mood, her soccer game always suffered. Since she wasn't the best athlete in the fifth grade to begin with, it was vitally important for her to be in a good mood on game days.

On Saturday, Kaylee was in a really bad mood, and it was the final game of the fall season.

To make matters worse, her team was playing the number one team in the league, the Lasers. And Michael Black stood on the sidelines again—cheering on Brittany. What did Michael possibly see in her? Kaylee wondered. Michael was the cutest boy in the fifth grade, in Kaylee's opinion. He was tall, broad shouldered and had wavy, dark hair above mysterious eyes. Sure, Brittany was blonde and athletic and cute in doughy sort of way, but she seemed to have something nasty to say about almost everyone—except Heather and Michael. Why did it seem that the nasty girls were always the most popular?

"You'd better not blow it again, O'Shrimp!" said Brittany menacingly as they warmed up in front of their goal. "For once in your life, do something to help us win!"

"Like sitting on the sidelines," Heather chimed in. A few of the other girls snickered. Kaylee felt a lump in her throat. Her father's voice kept her from crying.

"All right, girls! Let's line up!" shouted Coach O'Shay enthusiastically as he approached from center field where he had been chatting with the referee and the Lasers' coach.

Kaylee bounced in and out during the first half, usually at halfback or defender. She sighed with relief at halftime, glad that she had done nothing to either embarrass herself or cost her teammates the game. The rest of the Green Storm had played well, too. Brittany had booted two impressive goals, which had tied the score. This had left the Lasers clearly frustrated.

"Keep it up, Green Storm!" said Coach O'Shay as they gulped water or sport drinks. "You can win this one!"

They put their hands together and roared a team cheer that would have brought down the roof if it had been an indoor game. For the first time all season, Kaylee felt like she was a part of the team.

The score remained tied in the second half. The Lasers began to double up on Brittany, and she was unable to get free for a clear shot—except for one that bounced off the top bar at the front of the net. Remembering their last practice, Kaylee had smiled to see the ball bouncing right back toward Brittany.

While the Green Storm had trouble mounting much of an offense, the Lasers had their own difficulties. Heather and Naomi had played brilliantly at the defender positions, and with six minutes remaining, the score was still knotted at two. At a break in the action, Coach O'Shay signaled for substitutions. "Kaylee, Jackie, go in at the forward positions. Have Brittany move to halfback. You may be able to draw some of the defenders away from her." She glanced at Jackie and noticed her look of wide-eyed astonishment—a look that Jackie no doubt was seeing on Kaylee's face as well.

When Kaylee jogged onto the field and informed Brittany, she snarled darkly. "Your daddy must not want us to win the game if he's putting you two losers up front."

For once, Kaylee couldn't help but feel that Brittany was right. Her father should have put the fastest, most skilled players up front for a last big scoring effort. She and Jackie certainly did not fit that description.

But as the clock ticked down, Kaylee noticed that the Lasers were unable to move the ball past midfield. The Green Storm had too much talent in the backfield. *Well, at least it looks like we'll tie the best team. That's pretty good.*

"One minute!" shouted the Lasers' coach, exhorting his players to get the ball downfield. They succeeded in getting it past the midfield line and one of the Laser forwards brought it toward the right corner. Naomi, however, stole the ball and sent a monster kick back upfield.

Right toward Kaylee.

Kaylee fielded the ball and turned. A Laser defender stood just a few feet away, a pillar of menacing athleticism. Kaylee took a deep breath. *This is where I blow it.* She made a feint to her left and dribbled right, leaving the defender behind. *Wow!* she thought. *That worked better than I expected.* There was one more defender to beat, but Kaylee knew better than to hope she would get lucky twice. She kicked the ball toward Jackie, who was coming up the left side. Unfortunately, Kaylee's pass wobbled lamely in not quite the right direction. Although the Laser defender got in front of it, the ball bounced off her shin guard and back toward Kaylee.

She had only a split second to react. The Laser girl was almost on her.

"O'Shay!" screamed Brittany, coming into view on Kaylee's right. "Pass it to me!"

Brittany was the team's top scorer. She was the one you wanted to have the ball for a last shot. But two Lasers were closing fast on Brittany. Jackie was still on the left side, wide-open.

Kaylee tapped a lob pass over to Jackie, who at first seemed surprised. However, she suddenly realized her position, right in front of the goal. Jackie spun to her left and lofted a shot toward the right corner. The goalie moved left, too, but not fast enough. The ball floated just over her fingertips and hit net.

Three whistle blasts sounded. Game over.

Kaylee's teammates jumped up and down, jubilant. Then they swarmed Jackie, giving her hugs, high fives, pats on the back. A few even gave Kaylee high fives, acknowledging her assist.

Coach O'Shay joined them at mid-field, like a big kid, unable to contain his own excitement. Then they lined up to shake hands with the Lasers before heading back to their sideline, where Kaylee's father spent far too long telling them how proud of the team he was. Almost no one seemed to mind.

As everyone collected their water bottles, warm-up pants and miscellaneous equipment, Jackie approached Kaylee. "Thanks," said Jackie. "That was my first goal. Ever. I never thought I'd score it against the best team."

"It was a sweet shot," Kaylee told her friend, smiling. "You looked like a pro."

"Maybe we can do a sleepover or something next weekend," said Jackie. "I'll call you." Then she trotted off toward the parking area where Mrs. Kizobu waited.

Kaylee noticed her father now heading toward the parking lot, dragging the equipment bag behind him. Kaylee tossed her water bottle into the duffle in front of her and got to her feet. She was surprised to find Brittany and Michael standing beside her.

Kaylee felt herself blush but tried to act casual and smiled pleasantly. "Great game, Brittany."

Brittany glared at her. "I'll remember that, O'Shrimp!" growled Brittany.

The smile evaporated from Kaylee's face. "Remember what?"

"Remember how you cheated me out of my third goal!" said Brittany. "You had the ball and I was right there beside you."

"But," protested Kaylee reasonably, "you were covered." She looked toward Michael, hoping that he might confirm this observation, but Michael simply stood there looking handsome and bored with the whole situation.

"You passed the ball to Jackie," said Brittany, saying Jackie's name as if she were talking about some contagious disease. "It was a close game and you had a choice between Jackie and me. No one with an ounce of brains would have passed it to someone like her if they could have passed it to a really good player."

"But," said Kaylee more meekly, "we won the game. Jackie made the goal."

"If anyone other than your daddy was coaching this team, you'd be sitting on the sidelines," Brittany continued, oblivious to Kaylee's words. "Making stupid passes to your favorites rather than doing what's best for the team. What a loser." Then

Brittany turned and walked away, Michael following a step behind.

Kaylee, shaking with anger and embarrassment, watched them go.

"But you were covered!"

Seven

Saturday afternoon, Kaylee felt angry about what Brittany had said to her after the soccer game.

Saturday evening, she felt angry because, despite her calculated politeness and flawless reasoning, her parents had not budged on the issue of Irish dancing.

"One word," her father had said, turning his pants pockets out as a visual aid. "Money."

Sunday afternoon she felt angry because she had promised to spend two hours in her grandmother's room. "We can do this every Sunday," her grandmother told her, smiling. "Won't that be fun?"

Kaylee had smiled the distant cousin of a smile in reply.

They had begun by paging through magazines and quilting books. The variety of patterns and the beauty of the finished quilts surprised Kaylee. She noticed that if you looked at the individual scraps that made up the quilt, they were often ugly and unimpressive. However, expertly combined, they created fabulous patterns. They bookmarked several possibilities and then began taking stock of the fabric box. *I guess this isn't terrible,* Kaylee thought.

"Did you want to see a finished quilt?" asked her grandmother excitedly. Kaylee nodded and Grandma Birdsall reached into a basket on the floor near her chair. The quilt she brought out was the size of a window, a mix of triangular and rectangular scraps that formed patterns of autumn colors surrounded by a border the color of a caramel apple.

"Did you make this?" asked Kaylee, her eyes admiring the immaculate stitching. Grandma Birdsall beamed, turning over a corner of the quilt to reveal the initials KB stitched into the backing.

"Kitty Birdsall," she said proudly. "I've made dozens of these."

Then the phone had rung. Kaylee could hear her mother speaking to the caller from the next room.

"Oh, hi Jackie! Uh-huh. Yes, Kaylee's here, but she can't talk just now. She's working with her Grandma Birdsall. Uh-huh. On a quilt." The conversation had gone on for a few more moments, and it had torn Kaylee up inside. The temptation to leap up and run to the phone, to abandon the cluttered lilac room where time moved at the pace of a turtle dragging another larger turtle up a turtle-proof mountain was immense. Her grandmother heard the call, too. Although she said nothing, she could see by the look in her grandmother's eyes that Grandma Birdsall expected her to leave.

And so Kaylee could not do it.

"I'll see Jackie at school tomorrow," Kaylee said, managing a smile with a Herculean effort.

Grandma Birdsall beamed at her granddaughter, and Kaylee was almost glad that she had said it.

Almost.

When Monday morning rolled around, Kaylee felt even more angry than she had over the weekend. This was because A: She felt like she had wasted the whole weekend, and B: Mondays always irritated her, because they meant five more days until another weekend.

On the bus ride to school, Kaylee told Jackie what Brittany had said to her after Saturday's game.

"Maybe you should tell someone how she picks on you," suggested Jackie.

Kaylee shrugged. "I told my dad at the start of the season."

"And?"

"He told Brittany to knock it off," said Kaylee. "Told her we're all a team, that we've got to work together."

"What did Brittany do?" asked Jackie.

"She called me a snitch," said Kaylee. "Told me it didn't surprise her that I went crying to daddy. So I didn't tell him about it after that."

Jackie frowned, lowered her voice so that others on the bus would not hear. "If I weren't such a wimp, I'd do something vicious to that girl!"

Kaylee gave her friend a look of amused surprise. "Like what?"

"I don't know," Jackie sighed. "I'm not very good at coming up with vicious plans."

Kaylee laughed. "It's because you're too nice of a person. Unlike you-know-who."

After the bus deposited the girls at school, they went to their separate homerooms. As the day ticked away, Kaylee found herself thinking about what Jackie had said. A vicious plan. The idea appealed to her. Not anything really vicious, like dynamite or poisonous snakes, but a plan that would put Brittany in her place. Instead of sitting back and letting Brittany abuse and embarrass her all the time, it would be nice to go on the offensive for a change.

However, no plan came immediately to mind—except for several involving dynamite and poisonous snakes—and finally, seemingly against the laws of nature, the school day ended.

Beth O'Shay arrived home later than usual that evening and glanced at the clock above the stove as she swept into the kitchen. "It's late. I'll have to make something that's quick." She stepped to the pantry, eyed the shelves, sighed, pulling out a box. "How's macaroni and cheese sound?"

"Yum," said Kaylee, and her mother set to work.

As Kaylee set out plates, she noticed that her mother seemed to be lost in thought. The water had begun to boil, but Mrs. O'Shay was simply staring at the box of pasta.

"Mom?"

Beth O'Shay blinked, looked up, embarrassed.

"Is everything okay?" asked Kaylee.

Her mother nodded uncertainly. "I guess now is as good a time as any to talk to you about this."

Kaylee wondered whether one of her teachers had called about a bad grade on a test or an assignment.

"Have you ever heard of Tr—" Beth O'Shay stopped short, put down her stirring spoon and went to her handbag, which she had left hanging on the door knob. She fished inside and withdrew a piece of paper.

"Trean   Gaoth?"   said   Mrs.   O'Shay, pronouncing the words the way one might disarm a bomb—"TRY-an GAY-uth".

Kaylee wrinkled her nose. "What's that?"

"A school," explained her mother. "A dance school."

"A dance school?" repeated Kaylee, wondering where this was going.

"Trean Gaoth Dance Academy," said Mrs. O'Shay, reading from the brochure in her hand. "Irish dance. It's in Paavo, about ten miles from here."

Why bring this up? wondered Kaylee. *Are you just trying to torture me?*

"I hope you don't mind," continued her mother, "but your father and I, well, we signed you up."

Kaylee blinked. "Signed me up? What do you mean?"

"For lessons," said her mother, smiling thinly. "You start this Thursday."

Kaylee stood dumbfounded, hardly able to believe what she was hearing.

"Oh, honey," said Mrs. O'Shay, mistaking her daughter's shocked expression for disappointment. "We thought this was what you wanted."

Kaylee ran to her mother and embraced her. "Oh, it is! Thank you!" Tears flowed down her cheeks. "But the money. How will you and dad afford this?"

Mrs. O'Shay stroked her daughter's hair. "Don't worry. Sometimes you just find a way."

Eight

It seemed to take forever for Thursday to arrive. In the days beforehand, Kaylee tried on dozens of combinations of shorts, t-shirts and sweat pants. What did Irish dancers wear for practice? She did not want to look like a complete geek.

"You look fine," said her mother each time Kaylee emerged from her room modeling another potential workout combination.

Kaylee's group began its practice at 6 p.m., but Mrs. O'Shay arrived fifteen minutes early. Trean Gaoth Dance Academy was located in Paavo's downtown in a brick building that, according to Kaylee's mother, had been a bowling alley until eight years ago. Weeds grew alongside the building and an older woman in a shabby gray overcoat stood outside puffing on a cigarette. Kaylee could tell by the concerned look on her mother's face that she had expected something more elegant, a building with an exterior that said "dance" rather than "beer and pretzels". "Oh well," she muttered, seeing the wide smile on her daughter's face. She parked near a dozen others cars.

A long wooden sign bearing the academy's name hung above the double glass entrance doors. As they approached, the older woman with the cigarette looked up, exhaled an enormous cloud of smoke and grunted a nod in their general direction. This seemed to startle Kaylee's mother, who stopped in her tracks, her eyes suggesting that she might flee to the car. Kaylee, however, tightened her grip on her mother's hand and succeeded in drawing her past the woman who had now turned to blow another cloud away from the entrance.

Stepping inside, Kaylee and her mother found themselves facing a wide dance floor that had been built over the eight bowling lanes. The former bar area to their left had been partitioned into offices.

Several dozen girls who looked to be between five and nine years old were changing into street shoes, having just finished their workout. Some were saying goodbye to a red-haired woman who appeared to be in her early- to mid-twenties. Kaylee's mother, who seemed to have regained most of her composure, headed in that direction.

"Hi," she said, extending her hand. "Are you Annie Delaney?"

"I'm Tara." Kaylee felt certain the teacher was looking at her workout clothes as if she had worn the most devastatingly inappropriate things imaginable. As Tara stepped forward, Kaylee guessed she would be ordered home to change. Instead Tara smiled and shook her hand. "I guess we have a new recruit?"

Kaylee nodded bashfully, making a mental note that Tara was wearing Spandex shorts and a white t-shirt.

"This is my daughter, Kaylee," said Mrs. O'Shay. "I spoke with Miss Delaney on the telephone a couple days ago."

A voice called out from behind them. "Hello!" They turned to see a tall woman, about thirty-five, with waves of golden hair tied back in a ponytail and penetrating green eyes behind smallish, oval eyeglasses. She wore navy-blue warm-up pants and a gold and navy-blue Trean Gaoth t-shirt. Kaylee had expected the owner of the school to be much older. Miss Suzie had been nearly sixty and nowhere near as fit-looking as Annie Delaney.

"Miss Delaney," said Kaylee's mother, extending her hand again. "I'm Beth O'Shay."

"Call me Annie." The two women shook hands. "And this must be our newest student." She gave Kaylee a quick appraisal, shook her hand as well. "Have you done much dancing, honey?"

Kaylee replied unsurely, "I danced for four years at Miss Suzie's."

"Ah," said Annie with a subtle smile. "Well, Irish dance is a bit different. I'm sure you'll pick things up quickly, though. Tara will be teaching your daughter's class along with my other full-time instructor, Helen." Annie craned her neck to look across the dance floor. "I don't see Helen right now, but Kaylee will meet her later. I also have several other part-time instructors who supervise various classes. The class that Kaylee will be starting is for beginner dancers. Once they reach a certain level, they get bumped to a more advanced class."

She paused, assessing Kaylee's attire. "Does she have dance shoes?"

Kaylee opened her zippered duffel, pulled out the old ballet shoes she had used in her last year with Miss Suzie. They had been pretty tight when she had tried them on at home.

"That'll do for tonight," said Annie dourly. "But Kaylee will need ghillies and, if she sticks with it long enough, hard shoes. I can show you where to buy new shoes or, if you don't want to make that kind of investment right away, there are always used shoes for sale."

Kaylee's mother nodded, but Kaylee could see that behind her eyes, the dollars and cents were being calculated.

"She'll also need dark shorts and a white t-shirt for practice," said Annie. "And, eventually, you may want to buy a new or used school dress."

"Do all the girls have to buy a school dress?" asked Mrs. O'Shay apprehensively. "Even the ones who just want to learn Irish dancing for fun?"

Annie answered matter-of-factly. "First of all, we want the girls to love Irish dance. But we want them to become good at what they're doing, too. As a result, we work hard, and many of the girls choose to participate in public performances and in feisanna." Annie pronounced this word FESH-uh-nuh. "In order to take part in these, you need a school dress. Kaylee could certainly choose not to be involved in the performances, and that's just fine. But I should tell you that Trean Gaoth Academy has more than three hundred dancers, and I'd say that ninety-five percent get the dresses."

Beth O'Shay bit her lip. Annie noticed her anxiety and gave her a comforting smile. "I'll give you all of the details in my office. Kaylee can get started with her first practice."

By this time, other girls had arrived and Kaylee watched as they laced up their soft dance shoes—the ones they called ghillies—and stepped onto the dance floor to begin their warm-ups. Their feet moved so quickly, so gracefully, not so differently from the dancers she had seen on TV.

What have I gotten myself into? Now Kaylee was the one who felt like running for the car. *I'm going to look foolish next to these girls. It's going to be just like soccer.* She wondered which of the girls out there now on the dance floor would become her Brittany Hall.

Kaylee's shoes stood out immediately, being white. All of the other girls wore black ghillies. She moved gingerly onto the dance floor and began doing some simple stretching exercises, feeling the stares of the other girls even without looking at them. Tara stepped to the middle of the floor.

"Girls, we have a new dancer with us tonight! Her name is Kaylee!"

The girls smiled, waved, offered meek greetings.

"All right!" Tara called. "Let's do group!"

The girls formed a circle around Tara and began imitating the stretches she demonstrated. This lasted for fifteen minutes or so. Some of the stretches were familiar, but even those that Kaylee had never tried before were easy to follow. So far, so good.

"We're going to start today by working on our jig!" said Tara. "Let's form two lines!"

Kaylee positioned herself in the second row. *What the heck is a jig?* This was where things would begin to get ugly. A deep voice suddenly boomed out behind her.

"What's this? A fresh recruit?"

Kaylee noticed a faint odor of cigarette smoke. She turned and discovered the same older woman she and her mother had passed on the way into the building. The drab overcoat was now gone, revealing gray sweat pants and a black t-shirt. She seemed to be six feet tall, had unevenly graying hair and looked broad enough across the shoulders to play linebacker in the NFL.

Kaylee stared at the enormous creature hovering above her, unsure whether the woman's facial expression should be interpreted as a sneer or a smile. *One thing's for sure,* thought Kaylee. *She's definitely not an O'Shay family descendant.*

"I'm Helen Cole," said the woman, giving Kaylee's hand a mighty shake after Kaylee had waited an entirely inappropriate amount of time to introduce herself. "You may call me Miss Helen."

This seemed to be a cue for the other girls, who offered a smattering of Hi-Miss-Helens.

At this point, Kaylee remembered her own manners and introduced herself.

"I'll be working with Tara to teach you these beautiful dances," continued Miss Helen matter-of-factly. Then her eyes scanned the group of girls. "Caitlin Hubbard!" Her voiced boomed like cannon fire.

A slim, chestnut-haired girl with large eyes, a long face and high cheekbones stood up. "You're going to help Kaylee today. You'll have to teach her the jig as we go."

The girl nodded and weaved through the dancers so that she stood next to Kaylee, shaking Kaylee's hand ceremoniously as she arrived. At this point, it became clear that she also possessed an enormous smile.

"Sorry to be a bother," muttered Kaylee.

Caitlin gave her a what-are-you-talking-about? look. "I went through the same thing when I joined four months ago. Now it's as easy as can be." Kaylee watched as Caitlin effortlessly danced the entire jig for her. Caitlin's arms were tight to her side, her shoulders back, her legs perfectly coordinated and graceful, like watching poetry.

"Wow," said Kaylee when Caitlin had finished. "You learned how to do that in just four months?"

Caitlin smiled broadly. "That's just one dance. You've got five more to learn, plus our performance routines!"

Kaylee swallowed hard. "I'll never be able to do that!"

"Sure you will," said Caitlin, still smiling. "I'll help you! And you really don't have to learn them all right away. In the first year, it's pretty much the jig and the reel."

"The what?"

Caitlin laughed. "You'll see."

For the first time since she had walked into Trean Gaoth Academy, Kaylee felt herself relax just a bit.

And for the first time, she felt that maybe she really could do this.

Nine

Her legs ached the next day. The first night's practice had lasted an hour and a half.

"Remember," said Tara as they left, "you should be practicing on your own at least four days a week."

If I practice on my own four days, I'll be in a wheelchair, thought Kaylee.

Despite the pain, she practiced in her room when she came home from school on Friday.

Her mother surprised her when she arrived home after work, setting a pair of ghillies in front of Kaylee at the supper table. "They're used," she apologized, "but they're your size. Molly Wolter's mother gave them to me. Molly used to dance, but now she's off at college and doesn't have time."

Kaylee hugged her mother. "They're great!" She tried them on and then danced until bedtime— with a short break for supper.

"Don't wear out those shoes in the first week you have them!" said her mother, only half joking.

"Don't wear out your bedroom floor!" added her father, and Kaylee sensed he was not joking at all.

Kaylee practiced for several hours on Saturday. On Sunday, she was exhausted and wanted nothing more than to sleep. However, her parents dragged her out of bed early to go to church. After lunch, she was ready for a nap. That's when Grandma Birdsall arrived at her bedroom door.

"Time for our weekly quilting party!" the old woman said brightly.

Kaylee was going to tell her she was too tired, but when she raised herself on an elbow from her bed, the look on her grandmother's face turned her into a coward. She slouched into Grandma Birdsall's room and suffered through the worst two hours of her life, barely able to keep her eyes open. It made her a little angry that her grandmother didn't seem to notice that she was teetering on the edge of a serious coma.

By Monday, Kaylee's feet were so sore she could barely walk.

"You never looked this bad after soccer practice," said Jackie as she watched her friend hobble to her seat on the bus.

"This was self-inflicted," said Kaylee.

Her second dance class at Trean Gaoth seemed easier than the first. Even though her feet still ached somewhat, now Kaylee was familiar with the routine. When they practiced the jig, she actually looked like she knew what she was doing, though she was nowhere near as smooth as her more experienced classmates. She also felt more comfortable because her ghillies matched those worn by the other girls. And having Caitlin there to teach her the new steps made her feel much less intimidated.

"You've really improved!" Caitlin told her with a big smile. "You must have done a little practicing!"

You have no idea how much, thought Kaylee.

Her legs burned during the stretching exercises.

"It'll get easier," promised Caitlin.

"It better," responded Kaylee.

Not only did they work on the jig, but also on a dance called a reel. "I can't wait to do hard shoe dances," said Kaylee, remembering the exciting staccato clatter from *Isle of Green Fire*. "They really look like fun!"

"Remember, girls don't start hard shoes until second year," said Caitlin.

During a water break near the end of the class, an exhausted Kaylee slumped onto the floor next to Caitlin. "How do you keep track of all the different steps?" She wiped the sweat from her brow. "I'm just on my second dance, and already I'm confused!"

Caitlin shrugged. "Somehow your brain eventually sorts it all out. Or it doesn't, and you go back to some simpler sport."

Kaylee sat up straighter, looked at Caitlin with some skepticism. "You think dancing is a sport?"

"Of course," said Caitlin without hesitation, flashing a bright smile. "It's hard work, isn't it? It requires muscles and flexibility, doesn't it? You have to practice hard to get good, don't you? And you compete against others, right? Sounds like a sport to me!"

Kaylee's eyes widened. "Compete? What do you mean?"

Caitlin seemed to not understand the question for a moment, but then she smiled. "You really are a rookie. There's more to Irish dancing than just taking classes. In a year or two, if you stick with it, you'll be doing feises." The last word came out FESH-iz.

Kaylee remembered that Annie had used the word feisanna and mentioned this to Caitlin.

"Feises, feisanna, same thing," explained her friend. "It's the plural of *feis*, an Irish dance competition. There's more than two thousand girls at some of them. You compete against dancers from all over the country and a judge ranks you."

Kaylee snorted. "I'll never be able to do that. I'd probably place two thousandth."

"You only compete against girls your same age and at your same level. You'll start at the beginner or maybe the advanced beginner level. Once you get good, you can move up."

"But," asked Kaylee, "you said I can't do feises for a year?"

"The first year, most girls just do group performances with the whole school," explained

Caitlin. "We dance our routines in sets or lines to music. You'll probably do the big show in Madison this spring!"

It sounded exciting. And what Caitlin had said about Irish dance being a sport made perfect sense, though Kaylee had never thought of it like that before. Hard work, strength, practice and competition—Irish dance really was a sport. Of course, soccer was a sport, too. Hard work, strength, practice . . . all of that applied to soccer, softball, gymnastics and other competitive activities. However, while practicing her Irish dances, Kaylee already felt something new and different. Now she understood how her father had felt about soccer all these years. She felt excited every time she laced up her ghillies, every time she stepped onto the dance floor, every time she daydreamed about Irish dance for half a second in school, as if someone had ignited a fire inside of her.

A green fire.

Like her father's passion for soccer, she hoped that this fire would burn for a long time.

Ten

Kaylee's room was not the ideal place to practice dance, but if she moved about carefully, she succeeded in getting a pretty good workout. Sometimes she bumped into the bed on one side, but she was careful to avoid coming into contact with harder items like her bureau or her desk. Carpet covered the floor of her room--not the best dance surface. However, her carpet had been worn down to a thin, smooth rag by years of traffic, so it was not the worst, either. According to Kaylee's mother, Irish dance had produced one extremely positive side-effect: Kaylee now kept the floor of her room picked up so that she could practice without breaking her neck.

Jump out hop back two-three-four, lift heel switch point lift one-two-three-four, switch point switch point lift one-two-three-four, lift step lift step lift one-two-three-four.

The music played in her head. The small size of the room was a minor problem. What she really wished for was the recorded music that her teachers used at the practices. She mentioned this to her mother when she arrived home from the Stitchin' Kitchen on Friday evening. Beth O'Shay, who had paused to put the groceries onto the kitchen counter, let out a small gasp and covered her mouth with a hand.

"I almost forgot," she said, opening the blue canvas tote she often carried to and from the store. She produced a CD in a plastic case. "Caitlin's mother—Mrs. Hubbard—stopped by the store. Seems like a very nice person. Said she had always wanted to stop in the Stitchin' Kitchen, said it looked like such a cute place, and now that our daughters were in dance together and friends, she had an excuse. She dropped this off."

Kaylee took the disk her mother offered. Written in marker on it were the words "Irish dance songs". Upon further inspection, Kaylee discovered a scrap of paper inside the case that listed the songs in order.

"Awesome!" cried Kaylee, running back to her bedroom. As she knelt on the floor to plug in her CD player, her mother arrived in the doorway behind her.

"Let's see you do one of your dances," said Beth O'Shay. "I don't think I've ever seen you do one from start to finish."

Happy to oblige, Kaylee consulted the list of songs, pushed a couple of buttons on her player and leaped to attention in front of her bed.

"Not here," said Mrs. O'Shay, giving the room a rueful look. "Let's go out into the living room where you'll have a bigger area."

Kaylee carried the CD player and found an outlet. The first number was the jig. Before the music started, Kaylee moved to the center of the room, bringing her arms straight down to her sides. She looked directly ahead, standing in first position. She stood steady as a statue for nearly the first eight bars of music, pointed her right toe and then launched into her steps.

Jump out hop back two-three-four, lift heel switch point lift one-two-three-four . . .

Her movements were crisp and precise—for the most part. She flubbed a step here and there, but she was pretty sure her mother would not notice. She glided, leaped, her toes pointed nicely. She finished and bowed as she had been taught, her right foot in front again. Point and bow. Mrs. O'Shay applauded.

"Wow!" said her mother, and Kaylee noticed a brightness in her eyes that she had not seen before.

She smiled proudly but then looked down at the gray t-shirt and tattered shorts she was wearing. "It looks better in shows, because then you're in costume."

As Kaylee looked up, she saw a guilty look on her mother's face. "I know you want a school dress," said Mrs. O'Shay. "We're working on it. Annie is trying to find a pre-owned dress that we can afford."

"I know," said Kaylee wistfully.

At just this moment, her father arrived home, hanging his keys on a hook near the pantry.

"Honey!" Beth O'Shay called to her husband. "You've got to come and see this! It's wonderful!"

Kaylee smiled but waved off the praise. "You should see the other girls, the ones who've been dancing for awhile."

"To dance so well after only a couple of weeks is very impressive," said her mother.

"Just wait," said Kaylee, "I'm going to practice every free moment I get!"

Mr. O'Shay stepped next to where his wife sat on the sofa.

"Do it again, sweetheart," Beth O'Shay instructed her daughter. "Show your father."

Kaylee eagerly found the right song and repeated the dance she had just done for her mother.

"Isn't she good?" Beth O'Shay asked her husband—who had settled next to her--when Kaylee had finished. "A natural!"

"Very nice," said her father, though Kaylee could not help but notice that his smile was not nearly as exuberant as her mother's—more of the "polite" variety, it seemed to her. Well, she asked herself, what could she expect? He was a dad, after all. Dads just didn't get excited about dancing the ways moms did.

Kaylee unplugged the CD player and headed for her room. Her father rose from the sofa, started toward the kitchen, but then suddenly turned back toward Kaylee, his eyes sparkling, a broad smile now spread across his face.

"Sweetheart," he called to Kaylee, who paused.

Maybe he really did like my dancing. She waited for the compliment.

"I almost forgot," continued her father. "I've scheduled some practices in the middle school gymnasium to get the team ready for the indoor season. Mondays and Wednesdays, six o'clock, starting next week! Pretty exciting, hey?"

Kaylee managed a smile.

"Pretty."

Eleven

It had been an exhausting week. Monday's soccer practice at the Four Mile Road Elementary School gymnasium had lasted for two hours. Kaylee and her teammates had gone through every drill they had ever practiced during the fall season, plus a couple of new ones that her father had either recently invented or picked up from a coaching buddy. As if this had not been enough to finish them off, he had then run them through a scrimmage that had lasted nearly half the practice.

"Wait until the indoor season gets started," her father had said to the girls at the conclusion of practice as they stumbled to the gym wall where their water bottles stood. "We're going to be better prepared than any of the other teams."

All Kaylee knew is that she was prepared for bed, and she could tell that her teammates felt the same way. However, she also knew that she had a good hour of homework waiting for her.

Wednesday had been a virtual repeat of Monday, except this time she had been sore before practice even started. When she finally collapsed next to her water bottle at the end of the ordeal, she wondered whether she would be able to get to her feet again.

"Maybe I'll just crawl to the car," she told Jackie, who lay in a heap beside her.

"Maybe I'll just let it run over me," Jackie added.

Because there was no way her body could recover from the two sessions of "Coach O'Shay's Death Camp" — as her teammates had come to call the practices — Thursday was the first day she had ever dreaded going to dance. On TV, she had seen people stagger to the finish after the Olympic marathon. Kaylee felt like that, but also like someone had dropped a piano onto her afterwards from a passing cargo plane.

"You seem sort of tired today," Caitlin told her.

"I have an incurable disease," replied Kaylee.

Caitlin looked stunned. "What is it?"

Kaylee sighed. "It's called My Dad." Then she explained about Coach O'Shay's Death Camps.

"Plus," Kaylee added, "I also practiced my Irish dancing during the week. Not as much as usual, though."

Caitlin offered her friend a weak smile. "Maybe it'll get easier after awhile. Have you talked to your dad about how exhausted you are?"

Kaylee shook her head vigorously. "No way. He'd just tell me that if I can't handle such a full load of activities, then I should quit dance."

"But you can't quit dance!" gasped Caitlin.

"No," agreed Kaylee. "I can't quit dance."

Later, when they began to go through their steps, Tara also noticed Kaylee's fatigue. When break time came and the girls went to their water bottles, Tara approached and gave Kaylee a good-natured tap on the bicep. "Looks like you're dragging a little today, Kaylee!"

Kaylee nodded and repeated what she had told Caitlin.

"Soccer!" said a gruff voice from behind Tara. Miss Helen had caught part of the conversation and now pounded her way into the group. "Soccer!" she said again, as if repeating the name of an intestinal parasite. "That sport's like quicksand! Sucks you in, and pretty soon you've got time for nothing else! You should get out while you still can!"

"I can't," said Kaylee softly, a bit unnerved at the severity of Miss Helen's reaction.

"Why not?" asked Miss Helen.

"My dad's the coach," Kaylee replied.

Miss Helen simply shook her head and walked away. Kaylee felt a little sick to her stomach the rest of practice and was certain she performed even more poorly. Afterwards, as they were changing out of the ghillies, Caitlin offered Kaylee a hushed explanation.

"You're not the first girl who's gotten the soccer speech. Miss Helen hates it!"

"I wish I had a soccer ball right now!" whispered Kaylee menacingly. "I'd kick it right at her head! What's her problem?"

"Lizzie Martin is her problem," said Caitlin. "You were lucky today. Sometimes she gives the whole Lizzie Martin speech. I've heard it several times. I'm sure you'll hear it eventually. Probably when some other new girl mentions soccer."

"Who's Lizzie Martin?" asked Kaylee.

Caitlin glanced around to see that Miss Helen was nowhere near. When she resumed speaking, she kept her voice low. "Miss Helen used to teach at a different dance school about fifteen years ago. Lizzie was her star. I guess Miss Helen spent bazillions of hours working with her. She was beautiful and athletic--"

"Miss Helen?" interrupted Kaylee. "That's hard to imagine!"

Caitlin rolled her eyes, but then saw by Kaylee's smile that the comment had been a joke. "Lizzie was the best at the school. According to Miss Helen, no one could dance like her. She was seventeen and had worked her way up to the championship level. Miss Helen figured she was certain to be top three at Worlds."

Kaylee repeated the word, puzzled. "Worlds?"

"The World Championships," explained Caitlin. "It's usually in Ireland or Scotland or something like that. It's every dancer's dream!"

Kaylee imagined how it would feel to stand on a stage in Ireland as people applauded you, acknowledging that you were the best on the planet. She felt a thrill of longing and excitement race through her. Then she remembered the story.

"So did Lizzie Martin become a world champion?"

Caitlin glanced around to see if anyone was eavesdropping and then shook her head. "Lizzie also played soccer two or three times a week, according to Miss Helen. I guess she was really good at that, too. Sometimes there were conflicts, and Lizzie usually chose soccer over dancing. It used to drive Miss Helen crazy. Then one summer, Lizzie got an opportunity to play on some traveling all-star soccer team. It was a big commitment."

"So?" prompted Kaylee.

"Lizzie decided she didn't have time for Irish dance anymore," said Caitlin, as if announcing the death of a close friend. "I think it really hurt Miss Helen. You know . . . you put your trust in someone, you give them your life, and then they just walk away."

Now Kaylee felt sorry for the mean comment she had made earlier about not being able to imagine Miss Helen as beautiful or athletic. The two girls finished putting away their shoes in silence.

The ride home from dance was quiet, too. Usually Kaylee bubbled away, describing what they had done at practice, mentioning silly things that Caitlin had said, repeating advice that Tara or Miss Helen had given them, describing new dance steps or drills. On this night, she said nothing. Her mother attributed this to the physical exhaustion that can accompany a busy week. And she was right. But Kaylee was also quiet because she felt that if she said anything, she might burst into tears. For the first time, she had not enjoyed dance practice. She had felt physically drained from the start, and when Miss Helen had spoken harshly to her about soccer, this had diminished a part of her spirit, too. It wasn't so much that she cared whether Miss Helen liked soccer. It was that Kaylee cared about whether Miss Helen liked *her*. For the first time, Kaylee felt that something might threaten her love of Irish dance, but she could not decide whether it was soccer or Miss Helen or something else entirely.

At home, Kaylee proceeded to her room where she tossed her shoe bag in a corner and flopped onto her back on her bed, still wearing her workout clothes. She barely had time to close her eyes when she heard a gentle tapping at her doorway. Opening her eyes, she raised her head just enough to see Grandma Birdsall standing there, smiling.

"I'm so glad you're home," said her grandmother, who took a step into the room, carrying several magazines in her arms. She seemed rather pleased with herself. "I was hoping we could go over some patterns tonight. Then we could get right to sewing on Sunday afternoon."

Couldn't her grandmother see that she was tired? Didn't the old woman have enough sense to know that this wasn't a good time? "I'm tired, grandma."

Her grandmother paused, still smiling. "I understand," she said, but then held out a magazine toward where Kaylee lay. "But if you could just take a quick peek at this one that I've got marked. I found it this afternoon and I knew it was the sort of thing you'd love."

Kaylee suddenly sat bolt upright in bed and shouted, unable to hold back. "Do you know what I'd love? I'd love to not have everybody telling me what to do! 'You've got to play soccer!' 'You shouldn't be playing soccer!' 'You've got to spend Sunday afternoons cooped up inside making quilts!' All my friends have lives of their own, but not me! They're at the mall and I'm stuck inside taking sewing lessons!"

Her grandmother seemed to get a little smaller right before her eyes. She lowered the magazine, her eyes sad and watery, and headed back through the doorway.

Kaylee flopped angrily backwards onto her bedspread, trying hard to convince herself that after all she had been through the past week, her reaction had been justified. But the words Caitlin had used to describe Miss Helen's feelings—"You put your trust in someone, you give them your life, and then they just walk away"—burned inside of her like fire.

Twelve

The weeks flew past, but that did not make them easy weeks. The soccer practices, if anything, became more demanding and intense. Kaylee continued to work hard in dance practices as well, not only on Thursday nights, but throughout the week at her home.

"I can't believe any of the other girls in your dance group practice more than you," her mother told her one afternoon as she watched Kaylee bounce around the living room doing her jig.

Her father, who was reading the newspaper in the same room, offered a grunt. "If she put in half as much time practicing soccer, she'd be an all-star."

Despite his skepticism about her dancing, even her father had to admit that it seemed to have a positive effect on her soccer skills. "Your feet seem faster," he said one day. "Ever since you started dancing, you've become a better ball handler."

Kaylee smiled, for she had noticed a difference, too. Not just in her ball handling, though. Her stamina had improved, and her legs looked stronger.

Even so, all the hard work exhausted her. Kaylee looked forward to the Christmas break, which started two days before Christmas Eve and continued until January 3rd. There were no dance or soccer practices scheduled during that time, and Kaylee needed the vacation to recharge her batteries. She also knew that after the holiday break, her routine would change from tough to impossible. In mid-January, the indoor soccer league season would begin. That would mean practices on Mondays and Wednesdays and games on Saturdays at an indoor soccer arena in Paavo. On top of that, Kaylee learned that her dance practices would increase. Annie had told the girls in her class that they would be starting two-per-week practices the second week of January in order to prepare for their St. Patrick's Day show in Madison. "These performances are very important," Annie had told them. "We want to look sharp, polished, professional. Thousands of people will be watching, and this is how they will judge our school!"

"I don't know why I'm working so hard," Kaylee confessed to Caitlin after one practice. "I don't have a school dress. You can't dance in soccer shorts."

"Maybe you'll get some money for Christmas, and you can start putting it aside with your birthday money until you have enough for a dress," suggested Caitlin.

Kaylee shook her head. The Santa that stopped at her house arrived in a wooden sleigh, not in a limousine. "Even if I added money I got for weeding our neighbor's garden, it'd take me fifty years to save up enough for one of those dresses!"

Caitlin thought for a moment, and then smiled, making the shape of a handgun with her thumb and index finger. "Well then, it looks like we'll just have to start knocking off convenience stores!" She blew across her raised finger as one might blow across the barrel of a recently-fired gun. Both girls laughed.

In addition to their Thursday dance class, Kaylee learned that her group would also practice on Sunday afternoons—which had been a sore subject ever since she had blown up at her grandmother.

Kaylee had tried to make things right. The day after she had lost her temper, Kaylee had come to Grandma Birdsall's bedroom. "Grandma," Kaylee had said, startling her grandmother who had been facing away from the open doorway, reading a quilting magazine. "I . . . I was in a bad mood yesterday."

Grandma Birdsall put down the magazine, looked kindly at her granddaughter. "Everybody has days like that, dear. Sometimes I can be a regular tyrant."

"I've never seen you get angry," said Kaylee meekly.

Her grandmother chuckled. "You should have seen it when your mother and I would disagree. When she was your age, she was sometimes impossible. One time she got angry because I made her clean her room. She slammed her door so hard that it knocked a picture off the living room wall. The glass shattered everywhere. Oh, was I mad!"

"I still can't imagine the two of you arguing," said Kaylee. Then she remembered why she had come. "But I was wrong to say what I did. I still want to sew on Sundays. When I said I didn't, it was just because I was sore and tired and mad at everyone."

Her grandmother nodded a sad little nod. "I think we'll take a break from the sewing for a bit."

"Grandma, I—"

"Until your schedule gets a little easier," continued her grandmother, as if Kaylee had not spoken. "That will be fairer to you."

Kaylee had reluctantly agreed, feeling worse than ever. Now, with dance practices scheduled on Sunday afternoons, it looked like there would be no sewing any time in the immediate future.

With the holidays nearing, Kaylee's father was putting in more hours at the hardware store. When he cancelled the upcoming Wednesday night practice because of work, Kaylee did not complain. In fact, she felt much more refreshed in dance practice on Thursday.

"Someone's feeling good today," said Tara, noting Kaylee's ready smile and the ease with which she moved around the dance floor.

Practice began as it always did, with stretching. To Kaylee, this always seemed to take forever. The first ten minutes of stretching were similar to what any athlete might do—working the calves, the hamstrings, doing straddles. Then Tara started a CD, usually popular music that one of the girls had brought. For the next ten minutes, their stretches were done in time to the music, like a kind of modified aerobic workout one might see at an exercise club. The loosening up, however, was now more specific to the dances they would be doing. It included skips, leap-overs and all the other basic dance elements.

Then Miss Helen would take over, which signaled the point where they worked their "abs"— the abdominal muscles—with leg lifts, sit-ups and "crunchies". Kaylee's grandmother had used the word "tyrant" the other day. Kaylee was pretty sure that if she looked it up in the dictionary, Miss Helen's picture would be next to it. *I wonder what kinds of exercises she had Lizzie Martin do?* Kaylee thought as she suffered.

After they were warmed up, Tara and Miss Helen would drill them in the basic movements— over and over and over. "Point the toes!" This would be followed by having them perform portions of the jig in unison. "Together! One-two-three, two-two-three!" Ultimately, they would move on to doing the entire dance. "Toes out!" They would repeat this for the reel.

Performing the whole dance was the part Kaylee loved best. As she stood rigid, toes out, arms like ropes at her side, she felt a kind of excitement build inside of her, like waiting for the engines to roar to life when a rocket was launched toward outer space. Then she would point the right toe in front and begin precisely on cue, gliding, leaping, feet moving intricately in precise accord with the music. The sound of the accordion filled her, and she felt herself carried not away, but *into* the music.

Each step, each turn seemed a part of the poetry of her imagination, something she could neither separate from herself nor disregard. Yet, she also remained completely focused, aware of the sensation of effort that had evolved into happiness.

She realized that she was not the only one who felt this way. They moved together, like a machine and yet more than a machine, for they were filled with oxygen and passion. Although they were individuals, they became something greater through their cooperation, the sort of something that would someday soon make audiences say, "Wow!" They became art.

And then the dance was over. She bowed, relaxed, able to appreciate the simple greatness in what she—what they—had just done. Like a wide receiver in football catching a long, beautifully-arching pass; like a basketball player sinking a three-pointer; like a golfer placing her shot a foot from the pin.

Kaylee smiled. *I love Irish dance.*

Thirteen

For the first time, Kaylee faced Christmas vacation with a tinge of sadness. Yes, she was looking at two weeks of sleeping in as late as she wanted, two weeks without homework, and, of course, Christmas itself.

However, she was also looking at more than two weeks without dance, which would not resume until the first Thursday in January.

"We don't have to wait that long to see each other," said Caitlin as the two of them talked about it after the final December practice. "We can have a sleepover." She turned to her mother, who was watching the girls change back into their street shoes.

"That sounds like fun," said Caitlin's mother. "Just find a date when we don't have something else scheduled. For instance, not Christmas Eve."

Caitlin flashed her mother a smile.

"My mom should be here soon," said Kaylee. "She usually carries her pocket calendar." Some of the mothers stayed to watch practices or talked amongst themselves while their daughters worked out. Mrs. O'Shay usually ran errands or sat in her car, reading. She came through the entrance a few minutes later, glancing about uncomfortably as she always did, as if the place were full of spiders. However, Beth O'Shay quickly agreed to the sleepover plan. After this, it was the two mothers who worked out the details.

"It looks like the Wednesday between Christmas and New Year's Eve will work," reported Mrs. O'Shay as the girls finished packing away their shoes. Kaylee and Caitlin squealed.

"It'll be at my house!" said Caitlin as their mothers coaxed them toward the exit. "Bring your ghillies!"

Both mothers rolled their eyes. "Don't you get enough of a workout at dance practice?" asked Mrs. Hubbard.

"Tara works us plenty hard," said Kaylee.

"And Miss Helen works us even harder," added Caitlin. "It's just that we love to dance!"

Mrs. O'Shay failed to suppress a smile.

"Time to go," Mrs. Hubbard said abruptly.

"I-M me later!" called Caitlin. "My screen name is—" She stopped, seeing the glare from her mother. Then she lowered her voice to a whisper. "Oops. Don't want everyone in the world to hear this!" She whispered in Kaylee's ear.

Kaylee flushed slightly. "I'm only allowed to use the computer for homework."

Caitlin frowned. "But we have to work out all the details of this sleepover!"

Caitlin's mother rolled her eyes. "Try the phone!"

They did try the phone, the result being that both mothers had to put time limits on their calls.

"You'd think," said Beth O'Shay, "that you two girls were planning six months in the Amazon rather than a one-night sleepover."

"It's not just us two girls anymore, Mom," Kaylee confessed. She explained to her mother that two other girls from dance class, April Lee and Megan O'Connell, had also been invited, and that Caitlin's mother had approved.

"She's a brave woman," said Mrs. O'Shay.

On Christmas Eve, it snowed, but not nearly as much as Kaylee had hoped. "Not even an inch," she frowned. "You can't even sled on it!"

"It still looks nice," said her mother.

They attended an evening service at their church, returned home for cookies and cider, and then began to settle down for the evening.

Grandma Birdsall had started to join the family on Christmas Eve after Grandpa had died, and it had become a tradition that she read *The Night Before Christmas* to the children at bedtime.

"Are you sure you want me to do it?" her grandmother asked, as a pajama-clad Will hopped onto the living room sofa beside her and handed her the old picture book. She looked up at Kaylee. "You probably feel like you're too old for grandma to read to you."

"No way, Grandma!" cried Will, snuggling against her shoulder. "You've got to!"

Kaylee, dressed in sweat pants and a t-shirt—her usual winter sleeping gear—sat on the other side of her grandmother and smiled pleasantly.

"'Twas the night before Christmas," began her grandmother in the soothing sing-song voice that she used when reading, "and all through the house, not a creature was stirring. Not even a mouse!"

The O'Shay home smelled like cinnamon. The colorful lights on the Christmas tree faded into a hazy background blur. The old Christmas story, from a book that had been read to Kaylee since before she was a year old, awakened nearly a decade of Christmas Eve memories in her.

Before she knew it, her head was pressed against her grandmother's shoulder. Kaylee wished she could make this moment last forever. However, in no time at all, Santa had gone up the chimney. "But I heard him exclaim ere he drove out of sight, happy Christmas to all, and to all a good night!"

Will was already asleep. Kaylee did not move for a minute, and her grandmother did not make a sound either. Finally, still snuggled against her grandmother's shoulder, Kaylee said, "I love that story, Grandma."

Her grandmother spoke slowly, with something in her voice that suggested a peaceful happiness. "I know you do." And after a long pause, she added, "I love you, too."

Will woke before anyone else the next morning, and eagerly hunted down his loot. His highlights included computer games and a plastic castle with two armies of knights.

Kaylee received a Chicago Storm soccer jersey, which she suspected had been her dad's idea. However, she also found a DVD version of *Isle of Green Fire*, a new pair of ghillies and two pair of white poodle socks, the kind dancers wore with their ghillies.

"With all the practicing you do, I'm sure Santa figured it wouldn't be long until you wore out the old shoes," said her mother.

Then Kaylee spied a larger box bearing her name. "Probably clothing," she murmured to her parents, testing its weight and giving it a shake. "The biggest boxes are always clothing."

When she opened it, however, Kaylee was in for a shock.

"A school dress!"

She lifted it out of the box. It was made of a stiff, navy-blue material embroidered with a gold, white and green Celtic pattern on the front panels. A gold panel covered the upper torso, and a white lace collar lay above this. As she turned it over, she found the back panel or cape that was common to most school dresses. Emblazoned upon this golden field was the Trean Gaoth logo: a dove rising above a stylized gust of wind, surrounded by a wreath of Celtic knot.

Kaylee hardly knew what to say. She looked up at her parents and Grandma Birdsall, her mouth trying to form words, but nothing coming out.

"Go put it on!" cried her mother, whose own palms were pressed over her mouth.

Kaylee did not need to be asked twice. She rushed to her room and discovered that the dress fit perfectly. The moment she slipped into the dress, it felt as if someone had waved a magic wand, making the dress a part of her. When she returned to the living room, her grandmother let out a small gasp. Her mother again covered her mouth with a hand and it looked like this time, it might not be enough to hold back the tears. Even her father looked impressed. "You're beautiful, Kaylee," he said. And to tell the truth, she felt beautiful.

Then, wondering why she had not thought of it before, she rushed back to her bedroom, brought out the CD player and her ghillies. After lacing them on, she danced the jig for them.

"Seeing you do it in the dress gives me goose bumps," said her mother.

Kaylee cued up the reel and danced that, too. After bowing, she ran the palms of her hands along the front of her dress, the most beautiful article of clothing that she had ever owned. "I'd better take it off before it gets dirty," she said almost reverently. She skipped to her room, admired herself in the mirror for a bit, and then bounced back into the living room.

"How did you afford it?" she asked her parents. The school dresses were generally ordered from a dressmaker in Ireland. Kaylee had hoped to someday get a secondhand dress, but this one was obviously brand new.

Her father said nothing, looked at the ceiling. Her mother said, "Don't worry about that. Just enjoy it!"

Kaylee laughed and raced back to her room.

She was already enjoying it.

The Wednesday after Christmas, Kaylee's mother dropped her off at Caitlin's house. Almost two inches of snow had fallen the night before. Kaylee lugged her sleeping bag and a duffel filled with what Mrs. O'Shay felt was enough clothing and snacks for the entire cast of *Isle of Green Fire*.

Caitlin met her at the door and gave her a hug. Kaylee noticed that the foyer was as large as the O'Shay family kitchen—and it featured a dramatic vaulted ceiling that seemed twice as high as the ceiling in Kaylee's house. She glanced into a den, a dining room and a sun room as Caitlin led her through the house. Every wall surface appeared to be covered with ornate wallpaper, and the furniture and knick-knacks seemed to have been arranged by a professional design team.

"April and Megan are already here," said Caitlin, opening a door to reveal steps leading downward. "We're sleeping in the basement."

Kaylee hoped there would be some furniture down there, or maybe a mattress on the floor. Even with her sleeping bag, spending the night on concrete did not appeal to her.

When they reached the bottom of the stairs, Kaylee's eyes grew wide. Caitlin's so-called basement was like no basement Kaylee had ever seen. Instead of brick walls and a bare concrete floor with a furnace set off in a dark corner, Caitlin's basement was as nice as the upper level of her house. Thick carpet covered the floor. The walls were papered just as nicely as upstairs, and a solid, cream-colored ceiling had canister lights set into it. Several rooms opened off of the big main room, which featured a massive brown pit sofa in front of the largest flat panel television set that Kaylee had ever seen. Windows as large as the picture window in Kaylee's living room at home looked out into Caitlin's backyard, though it was already dark and she could make out no details. Kaylee knew, however, that it would be beautiful in the light of day.

"You can walk right out of your basement!" said Kaylee, pointing to a set of French doors between the two windows.

"The house is built into a little hill," explained Caitlin. "We can go sledding in the morning!" Then she pointed to a spot behind the pit sofa. "You can toss your sleeping bag here. We'll roll them out later. Mom's just about ready to serve the pizza."

Kaylee exchanged quick hugs with April and Megan, and then followed her three friends back up the stairs. Caitlin climbed directly in front of Kaylee, and it was at this point that Kaylee noticed the odd blue shoes she was wearing. They looked like a cross between running shoes and hiking boots, but the thick black sole was in two pieces with a gap between the heel and the forefoot.

"They're special practice shoes for dance," explained Caitlin when Kaylee inquired in the kitchen. "We were going through some of our dance steps before you got here."

Kaylee looked again at the shoes. "They're really cool looking. How do they feel?"

"Great," said Caitlin. "They really protect your feet!"

"But they really damage your pocketbook," said Mrs. Hubbard, who had turned from the oven and was placing a pizza onto the island countertop next to Kaylee. Mrs. Hubbard was taller and thinner than Kaylee's mom, and had straight dark hair. However, she seemed to shower everyone with the same motherly affection. "That's the way it is with Irish dancing," she continued. "Everything's expensive."

Caitlin told the girls what the shoes had cost. April whistled. Kaylee felt certain her surprise had registered in her eyes.

"Then there's ghillies and hard shoes and lessons," added Caitlin's mother. "And special socks, and sock glue and makeup. The school dress is a biggie. And a smock to keep it from getting dirty at shows. And a dress bag to carry it in. Plus practice clothing. Someday, we'll probably have to purchase a solo dress. There will be entry fees for the competitions. And don't forget the gas money to take you to lessons and shows. I don't know where we'll get the money for it all." She shook her head, but she was smiling and patted Caitlin's hair as if to say, *Don't worry. You know we'll find the money somewhere.*

After supper, they danced for hours. Then they made popcorn, watched movies, laughed incessantly and talked about boys. The other girls went to school in Paavo, and so Kaylee did not recognize the names of the boys in their stories. However, it was still fun to listen, for it seemed that boys everywhere behaved the same. After listening to her friends for awhile, Kaylee mentioned Michael Black, which made her blush even though there was really no reason for her to do so. She told them about Brittany, too, and how she treated Kaylee at soccer. Even though her friends had never met either of them, they seemed to reach the same conclusion as Kaylee. "What does he see in Brittany?" squealed April. "She just sounds nasty!"

Sometime after two in the morning, everyone seemed to have drifted off to sleep.

Except Kaylee.

She lay in the dark, her sleeping bag rolled out on a section of the pit sofa, staring out one of the windows into a backyard that she could not see. She thought about her school dress, a beautiful thing, her most sacred possession.

And she thought about what Caitlin's mother had said. If Caitlin's mother was concerned about the cost of Irish dancing, then how could her own parents afford it? From the look of Caitlin's house, her parents made ten times the salary that Kaylee's parents made.

So how had Kaylee's parents been able to afford a brand new school dress?

When she finally fell asleep, Kaylee dreamed that her father had gone to Ireland to help her great-great-grandfather lower the roof another foot on the O'Shay family ancestral home.

Fourteen

The indoor soccer season began in January with a blowout. Fortunately, the Green Storm won, scoring ten goals to only one for the Wildcats. Brittany put four in the net for the Storm.

Although the scores were closer, the Storm won its next two games against the Stampede and the Gold Rush.

Kaylee's father was in such a good mood that he took the team out for pizza after the win over the Gold Rush. "It's still early in the season," he told the girls as they sat around a big table at Frankie's Pizza Den. "We've got seven games to go. But I think we have a chance at winning the league title. The important thing is for us all to work hard, pull together and really dedicate ourselves to becoming better soccer players."

Kaylee nudged him in the ribs and gave him a big smile, which seemed to remind him of something. "Oh, right, and we also want to remember to have fun!"

They raised slices of pizza to toast this excellent idea.

The following Saturday, the Green Storm lost to the Kickettes.

"The Kickettes lost their first game of the season," said Mr. O'Shay at the team's Monday practice in the middle school gym. "That means they're tied with us, three wins and a loss. We still have just as good a chance at the championship as anyone."

Then he put them through the toughest workout of their lives. They started by dribbling the ball around an obstacle course of orange cones. After that, they scrimmaged for half an hour. Finally, he made them do Kaylee's least favorite drill—toe touches. They raced up and down the gym floor, touching each line with their toes, then back to the start, then up to the next line, and so on. Kaylee felt as if she had run a marathon, and during the second water break, she wanted to kick a soccer ball at her dad's head. This time, there were plenty of balls. However, Kaylee didn't have the strength.

Dance practices seemed to be getting more demanding, too. Kaylee noticed her legs growing stronger. The soccer and dance workouts together seemed to have given her more muscle definition and improved her speed. This improvement went unnoticed by most of her teammates—until the fifth soccer game of the indoor season.

All of the indoor games were played at the Paavo Sports Complex, a huge fieldhouse enclosing three soccer pitches. Each field had spongy, blue-green artificial turf and was surrounded by a plywood and glass enclosure just like a hockey rink. Also like a hockey rink, the teams sat in boxes at the side.

The rules for indoor soccer were mostly the same as for outdoor, except that the ball was kept constantly in play by the walls, eliminating the need for throw-ins or most corner kicks. In addition, substitutions were made while the game was in progress, another similarity with hockey. The action never stopped in indoor soccer, and although it was more tiring, the excitement of it made Kaylee prefer it to the outdoor variety.

Heather scored a goal in the first two minutes, but at halftime, the Green Storm and the Yellow Clash were tied with a goal apiece. Kaylee's father had warned them about the Clash during Wednesday's practice. "They've got two wins and two losses," Coach O'Shay had explained, "but they lost one of those games when they were missing two of their best players."

Those two players—the twin Valentine sisters—had been playing at the forward spots and kept the ball in front of the Green Storm goal most of the first half.

"It's a miracle they only have one goal," said Jackie breathlessly as they gulped water near the bench.

The situation did not improve in the opening minutes of the second half. The Valentine sisters controlled the ball, kept it upfield, and then, after a nice pass, Chrissy Valentine scored. Three minutes later, Debbie Valentine lofted one into the net. Chrissy scored again on a free kick following a hand ball four minutes later. At this point, Kaylee's father did what he had done during the outdoor season against the Lasers. He moved Heather and Brittany to defensive positions, inserting Jackie and Kaylee at forward.

"That's just stupid!" hissed Brittany as they jogged into position for the start of play. "What does he think he's proving? Is this supposed to be some kind of punishment because we're not scoring goals?"

"You two are our best ball handlers," noted Jackie, overhearing Brittany's complaints. "Coach probably wants someone who can challenge those Valentine girls and get the ball upfield for us. That's why he moved you back."

Brittany snorted. "Like it'll do any good even if we do with you two at forward!"

Kaylee felt her cheeks redden.

As play resumed, it became clear that Coach O'Shay's changes had made a difference. Brittany and Heather gave the Valentine sisters all they could handle, preventing them from getting a clear shot on goal. They also succeeded in booting the ball to the forwards, where Jackie and Kaylee tried to set up a shot on goal.

The minutes ticked by. Although Kaylee and her friend were able to control the ball fairly well, the Clash defenders moved like lightning and rarely were drawn out of position. The Green Storm's best scoring opportunity came on a free kick with ten minutes to go.

"You take the kick, Kaylee!" called her father from the sideline.

Kaylee had never tried a free kick in a game. Usually Heather or Brittany got the call. As the referee set the ball in front of the goal, Kaylee took a few steps backward, glanced up at her teammates to see if they were set. Jackie and another girl were bobbing back and forth along either side of the goal. Kaylee exhaled deeply, brought herself to speed and gave the ball a thundering boot—right into the wall where it rebounded and was controlled by a Clash player.

"Good try, Kaylee," yelled Jackie, as they jogged into defensive positions.

It hadn't been a bad kick, thought Kaylee. Good power. Just slightly to the left. As she backpedaled, Brittany's voice rang out behind her.

"Too bad we don't have some better players up front!"

"Subs!" The second voice was her father's. Kaylee turned, expecting to be called to the sidelines, but instead, she saw her father motioning to Brittany.

"You!" said Coach O'Shay, first pointing and then indicating the sidelines with his thumb. "Take a rest!"

Brittany looked like she had been doused with cold water. "There's only ten minutes left! I don't need a break!"

"Out!" said Coach O'Shay, his voice more menacing this time. He turned to Tina, a smaller girl who had been standing beside him. "You're in!"

Brittany's eyes grew dark. "You need to keep me in! We can still win!"

"I certainly expect us to try," said Coach O'Shay forcefully. "But I won't have you out there tearing down your teammates! Take a rest and think about it!"

Now the anger rose within her. "You can't do this!"

Coach O'Shay folded his arms across his chest and spoke in as calm a voice as the situation would allow. "Unless you're off the field in the next five seconds, you'll watch our entire next game from the sidelines!"

Brittany's face congealed into an ugly, twisted mass, but she jogged into the box. Tina replaced her, quickly intercepting the ball and sending it back upfield.

Kaylee suddenly felt very light on her feet, and she noticed that she was smiling, though just slightly. Her father had benched Brittany. How cool was that? Then the ball was in front of her. As a Clash defender closed in, she spotted Jackie cutting across the middle. Kaylee hit her with a perfect pass. Jackie accelerated toward the goal and brought her foot back with what Kaylee thought would be a shot at the net. Instead, Jackie tapped the ball back to Kaylee who had continued up the left side. Predictably, a Clash girl closed on her immediately. Instead of tapping back to Jackie, who was now covered, Kaylee bounced the ball off the wall on her left side. She cut around to the right of the Clash player and controlled her own pass, noticing immediately that she now had only the goalie to beat. One more step . . . kick . . . into the right corner of the net!

"All right!" shouted Coach O'Shay.

Her teammates rushed in, gave her hugs and high fives.

"Still six minutes!" Coach O'Shay informed them. "Let's get another!"

On the ensuing kickoff, the Clash took the ball deep into Green Storm territory. They tried a couple of shots, missed, and then Heather sent the ball back upfield. Jackie immediately passed to Kaylee, who suddenly felt like she could do anything she wanted with the ball, as if it were controlled by wires or a computer chip. She beat one defender, then decided to use the wall again—but this time, the wall in front of her.

As two Clash girls closed, she sent a powerful shot that bounced off the wall a few feet to the left of the goal—right where she wanted it. The ball bounced back toward Kaylee, who had never stopped running and who met the ball almost precisely as it touched the synthetic turf. It took off like a rocket— right past the goalie and into the net!

More, wilder hugs.

"One more ties it up!" reminded Coach O'Shay. When he looked at Kaylee, she saw his eyes sparkle. Kaylee was glad to be able to make him proud of her. She was almost as glad to see that Brittany looked like she wanted to chew a hole through a rock.

With fewer than four minutes to go, the Green Storm began to look tired. The Clash controlled the ball and seemed content to kill the clock. Finally, with a minute and a half to play, the ball bounced past mid-field. Kaylee took it down the left side. Three Clash players converged on her.

They think I'm some big superstar because I scored those two goals, Kaylee thought. *So they're all coming after me.*

It was one of those things teams sometimes do in desperation, not considering the consequences of playing out of position. The result was that it left Jackie wide open in front of the goal. Kaylee lofted a chip shot to her and Jackie put it into the net with a header.

Kaylee thought her father was going to have a heart attack.

When the game-over horn sounded seconds later, Kaylee's father jogged out onto the field to hug his daughter.

"That was the best game I've ever seen you play!" he said, his eyes wet at the corners.

"Thanks, Dad," said Kaylee.

She joined her teammates, shook hands with the Clash players. Then the Green Storm players met at their bench, joking, re-telling the game's great moments, shouting the sorts of things that athletes shout after a good game. Only one thing seemed to be missing.

Brittany.

When Kaylee looked around, she saw her from a distance, walking toward the exit.

Some team spirit, thought Kaylee.

Fifteen

The good news: Starting in February, Kaylee's weekends became a little less crowded. Annie announced that practices would no longer be held on Sunday afternoon for Kaylee's group. They would be rescheduled to another day.

The bad news: The new practice day turned out to be Monday, which meant a conflict with her soccer practice.

"Dad is going to have a meltdown when he finds out," Kaylee said dolefully to her mother on their way home from the Sunday practice at which Annie had given them the news.

Her mother had answered matter-of-factly. "I'm sure the two of you will be able to work out something."

Kaylee was not so certain.

When she finally told him at the dinner table that evening, she could tell before he spoke that he was upset. She noticed his nostrils flare slightly, his jaw tighten almost imperceptibly. He put down his fork and crossed his arms on the edge of the table just in front of his plate.

"I see," he said--the way people say it not when they understand, but when they don't.

"We've only got four games left," observed Kaylee reasonably. "I can get by with just one practice per week."

Her father regarded her skeptically but spoke in as level a tone as he could. "I'm glad you're so confident. I'm not. But even if I agreed with you, that's not the problem. Everyone else on the team will be practicing two days a week while the coach's daughter is only practicing once. Won't that look nice?"

"Dad," said Kaylee, her voice rising slightly in spite of her efforts to control it, "I made a commitment to train for our big show in March!"

A look of modest surprise appeared on her father's face. "It seems to me that you made a commitment to the Green Storm, too! But somehow that doesn't ever seem to count. Whenever you have plans, soccer always comes in second place."

"But Dad," cried Kaylee, "this is something I really, really want to do!"

Mr. O'Shay shook his head, staring at his half-empty dinner plate. "After the game against the Clash, I thought you'd forget all this other silliness."

"It's not silliness!" shouted Kaylee.

"Your voice!" said her mother, putting a finger to her lips.

Slurp, went her brother, who carried on as if he were dining alone.

Her father continued. "Kaylee, you were unbelievable out there. You handled the ball like a champ, you knew when to dish, and your two goals were spectacular. And don't tell me you weren't pumped up afterwards! Everybody giving you high fives, even the other parents telling you how well you did!"

"I don't see why we need two practices a week," said Kaylee in a more subdued tone. "Lots of other teams only practice once. Ashley Burke's team, the Vortex, only practices on Wednesdays."

"The Vortex is in last place," her father responded. "We have a chance to win the league, Kaylee!"

Kaylee had no intention of giving in. "But this will be my first performance with Trean Gaoth! Besides, Mom has already paid for the dance practices!"

"That was before they were switched from Sunday to Monday," noted Mrs. O'Shay.

"But they're still paid for," Kaylee pointed out. "The day is just different."

Mr. O'Shay looked to his wife, who shrugged helplessly. "She has a point," said Mrs. O'Shay. "We probably can't get a refund."

"So if I miss Monday dance practices, we're wasting our money," said Kaylee triumphantly. "But if I miss soccer practice, it doesn't cost us anything!"

Her father looked at Mrs. O'Shay, and then back at Kaylee, his face sullen and defeated. "I disagree," he said finally, rising from the table. "I think it costs a lot more than you think." Then he took his plate to the sink. Kaylee's mother followed him, leaving Kaylee, her grandmother and her brother at the table. Will had eaten nonstop through the discussion and showed no signs of slowing. Her grandmother had picked at her food, taking tiny bird-like bites, pretending that nothing more contentious than the weather was being discussed.

Kaylee looked at her own plate and realized that she had hardly eaten anything. She poked at a mound of mashed potatoes with her fork.

"So," said Grandma Birdsall after a long silence, "your dance schedule has been changed."

Kaylee knew where this was headed. Having heard that Kaylee no longer had dance practice on Sunday, Grandma was ready to pounce, to drag Kaylee back into the Sewing Zone, where time seemed to run backwards. Not willing to face this conversation in her current mood, Kaylee pushed away from the dinner table and huffed to her room.

Almost as soon as her door closed, she began to regret her action. All her grandmother wanted was someone to sew with. Kaylee opened her door a crack and looked across the living room to the kitchen. Will remained at the table, his lips smacking, oblivious to the world around him. Grandma was gone. When Kaylee looked down the hall, she saw that Grandma Birdsall's bedroom door was closed.

Kaylee felt a little pain in her stomach. *I'm selfish, I'm letting down my team and I'm disappointing my dad. I must be just about the world's worst daughter.*

As her eyes traveled back to the kitchen table, she saw her brother's head snap up suddenly in mid-chew, looking at something other than his own food. Then he called out loudly, "Dad! Mom! Kaylee didn't clear her plate!"

So I'm a slacker, too, thought Kaylee. *Now I'm definitely the world's worst daughter.*

Sixteen

Kaylee felt guilty all through Monday's dance practice. *My soccer teammates are working their tails off, probably wondering why I'm not there.* Part of her guilt came from a distressing suspicion that her father was right, that he would no doubt feel embarrassed that his own daughter was missing. Some of them would have asked him where Kaylee was. He would have told them the truth, and then he would have been forced to endure the whispers and the angry eyes—not from everybody, but from a few. That would be enough, though, to make him feel awful. And then Kaylee herself would have to endure the same whispers and looks when she returned to soccer practice on Wednesday. She could hear them already. "How come she got an easy day when we had to work our butts off?"

On the other hand, Kaylee could not imagine how the soccer team could have worked any harder than she and her dance teammates were working. Tara and Miss Helen put them through their stretching, drills and performance routines with the intensity of boot camp sergeants. By the time they reached the first water break, Kaylee was panting, her t-shirt damp with sweat. She told Caitlin about the argument with her father.

"It makes me wonder," said Kaylee as she concluded her story. "I mean, my dad is the coach. We could win the league championship. And my family really doesn't make the kind of money you need to make if you're going to be an Irish dancer. Maybe I'd be better off just playing soccer."

"Whoa!" said Caitlin, her eyes wide with startle. "We've talked about this before! You can't quit dance!"

Kaylee snorted ruefully. "Give me one good reason."

"I'll give you three," said Caitlin immediately. "First, you're good at Irish dancing!"

Kaylee was about to tell Caitlin that she had scored a few goals as a soccer player, but Caitlin hushed her with an index finger to the lips before continuing. "Second, you're my friend and I'd miss you!"

This made Kaylee smile. "What's the other reason?"

Caitlin returned the smile. "You love it. That's the most important one of all."

She was right, Kaylee had to admit. Kaylee liked how soccer was something she could do with her dad, and it had been a thrill to score goals in the game against the Clash. With dance, however, Kaylee felt the thrill constantly. She felt excited before every practice, the way a person gets excited when she is getting ready to go to a birthday party or a theme park or on a family vacation. She felt excited whenever she tried on her school dress—and she usually did this three or four times a week. Sort of like a superhero donning her costume. And when she thought about doing without soccer, it made her sad to think how it would hurt her father if she quit. It made her sad to think how she would miss sharing this time with him. But when she thought about eliminating Irish dance from her life, the idea completely devastated her, like her heart being wrenched out of her chest.

Kaylee felt better the second half of practice, and even though Tara and Miss Helen worked them even harder, Kaylee cruised through it all as if she really were a superhero.

"Whatever kind of vitamins you're taking, bring some for everyone next time," Tara joked with Kaylee as they finished up.

She arrived home a few minutes after her father.

"How was practice?" she asked sheepishly.

Her father nodded and, to her surprise, did not seem upset. "Better than I anticipated. Most of the girls understood your situation. There were just a couple who grumbled about it."

"Let me guess," said Kaylee, rolling her eyes. "Brittany and Heather."

"You got one right," said her father. "Brittany wasn't there. Haven't seen her since the Clash game."

Kaylee did not let her smile show on the outside. That would have been immature, and a show of poor team spirit, and taking pleasure from someone else's misfortune. Yet, she couldn't help feeling a little sunnier inside, though not simply because Brittany had fallen from the throne. She had imagined that her father might be in an awful mood after practice, that there would be a lot of yelling and hurt feelings, and that the evening would drag on forever. However, her father seemed to be okay with the arrangement now.

"After supper, I'll talk you through what we did at practice," continued Mr. O'Shay.

"Thanks, Dad," said Kaylee. "I mean, you're being really cool about this. I thought you'd be angry, you know."

Her father shrugged. "I wasn't happy. But the more I thought about it, the more I realized there was nothing to be done. And like you say, we do have two practices a week. It's not like you're skipping out of all the practices and then expecting to play in the games."

"And there's only four games," Kaylee added. "After that, we won't have to worry about dance conflicts anymore."

Her father chuckled. "Don't bet on it. You probably aren't going to stop dancing once you're done with your big show."

"No way," said Kaylee, shaking her head.

"And once the weather warms up, we'll start spring and summer leagues in soccer," her father continued. "So I guess I'd better get used to the fact that I've got to share you with the other love of your life."

Kaylee rushed forward and hugged him. "We won't have to worry about it for awhile," said Kaylee. "At least we'll have a break after these last four games."

Her father smoothed her hair as he held her to his chest. "And the tournament."

"Hm?" said Kaylee, bringing her face up to where she could see him.

"Four games and the season-ending tournament," said her father. "The ten games on our schedule determine who we play in the first round of the tournament. If we finish with the best regular-season record, we play the weakest team first."

Kaylee released her hug, thought for a moment. "Do we have the best record of wins and losses?"

Her father made the sort of face that people make when they mean "not exactly". "The Kickettes have only one loss. We've got a loss plus the tie with the Clash. But the Kickettes haven't played the Clash yet, and I think the Clash will beat them. If that happens, and if we can win these other four games leading up to the tournament, we'll probably get the top spot and play the team with the fewest wins."

Kaylee nodded faintly. "What happens if we win that tournament game?"

"We'll probably play two more games that same day," said Mr. O'Shay. "We'll have to win them all to win the tournament. And it will be very physically demanding, three games in one day. The first game starts at ten in the morning and the championship game isn't played until six in the evening. That's why I've been working you all so hard in practice. It's going to be a long day and you're going to have to be in top condition! But we've still got plenty of time to get ready. The tournament's not until the seventeenth."

It took a moment for this to register. When it did, Kaylee's heart skipped a beat. Something like fear began to swell inside of her.

"The seventeenth of February?" asked Kaylee hopefully.

Her father laughed. "Of course not, you knucklehead," he said, playfully tousling her hair. "February 17 is only about a week away. The tournament is next month. March."

A small cry escaped from Kaylee and her eyes filled with tears as she realized the cruel coincidence. "But that's St. Patrick's Day!"

Her father frowned thoughtfully. "I guess that's right. I hadn't really given it much thought. I guess our green uniforms will fit right in." He gave a little laugh, but when Kaylee failed to join in, he continued. "Anyway, it should be a lot of fun."

"No!" cried Kaylee. "It will be awful!" And when her father still did not understand, she spelled it out: "That's the day of our big dance show in Madison!"

Seventeen

The argument with her father had been an awful experience, not because it had been loud and angry, but rather because it had been just the opposite. Somehow, a person could avoid feeling guilty about an argument when both sides were shouting at one another. When the disagreement was quiet and sad and impossible to resolve, there was no worse feeling in the world.

She had been feeling so good, so close to her father. And then she had learned that the event she had been looking forward to for months would conflict with the event her father had been looking forward to for months. It was like winning $5 million in the lottery . . . and then finding out that you were $10 million in debt.

"What are you going to do?" asked Caitlin as they changed into street shoes after their dance practice the following Monday. "You can't be in two places at once."

Kaylee sighed, realizing that she had unlaced the dance shoe on her right foot and then absent-mindedly laced it up again instead of removing the shoe. "Maybe I'll just run away."

"Ha, ha," said Caitlin humorlessly. "There's no way you'd ever miss that St, Patrick's Day show! You've worked so hard!"

"But my dad would disown me if I missed the soccer tourney," argued Kaylee. "He told me I owed it to my teammates, that I had to show some loyalty!"

"Was he talking about dance or soccer?" asked Caitlin wryly. Then an idea seemed to occur to her. "Wait! What time is your soccer game? Maybe you can do both?"

"It's not one game," said Kaylee, grabbing the old duffel bag she carried to practice and stuffing her shoes inside. "It's three!" Kaylee explained how the Trean Gaoth bus to the Madison dance performance would leave at about the time she was supposed to play her first soccer game and return during the soccer finals. "I've either got to do one or the other!"

As Kaylee dropped her head into her hands, Miss Helen finished talking with a couple of parents and drifted over to where the two girls were sitting. "You girls aren't talking about soccer again, are you?" she asked, wrinkling her nose—which looked as if it might have been broken at some distant past date—in displeasure. Miss Helen could be as warm and nurturing as their own mothers when necessary, but she could also project an intimidating iciness. Soccer always brought out the iciness.

"My dad's a coach," said Kaylee tentatively, and Miss Helen nodded, remembering their earlier conversation. "We've got a big game coming up."

Miss Helen snorted as if Kaylee had informed her that she had thrown a bag of snakes through the open window of an orphanage. "Big game," she said in a low voice. Then she knelt down next to the two girls so that Kaylee could smell traces of cigarette smoke. "Both of you are good dancers," said Miss Helen in a serious voice. "Kaylee, it's amazing how quickly you've progressed in just a couple of months. I'm very excited to see you dance in the St. Patrick's Day show." She paused for a moment, and a smile played at a corner of her mouth. "Do you know what Trean Gaoth means?"

Kaylee shook her head. Caitlin, however, raised her hand as if she were in school.

"It means *strong wind!*"

Miss Helen nodded. "Exactly. That's what our school is all about. Dance is powerful. It lifts you up, like a strong wind."

Both Caitlin and Kaylee nodded silently.

"You both have a special talent," Miss Helen continued. "Someday, you might be dancing in the Prizewinner category or even Champion. Don't waste your gifts on . . . on crude games." Miss Helen rose to her feet, and since they understood the sad look in her eyes, the two girls almost felt like giving her a hug. "Why run through the mud when you can dance on the wind?"   Then Miss Helen smiled and walked across the dance floor toward another group of chattering girls.

Caitlin sighed. "Glad I'm not you!"

"I wish *I* weren't me!" said Kaylee gloomily, jamming her water bottle into the duffel. "Anything I do will mean a horrible, painful, unpleasant death. Did I mention gruesome?"

Caitlin shook her head.

"A horrible, painful, unpleasant, *gruesome* death," Kaylee amended herself and sat back against the wall. "Well, at least things can't—"

"Don't say it!" interrupted Caitlin.

Kaylee looked surprised. "Don't say what?"

"Don't say 'Well, at least things can't get any worse'," warned Caitlin. "Because whenever people say things can't get any worse, they usually do."

Unfortunately for Kaylee, she did not have to say it. On Wednesday, things got worse without any prompting from her. The Green Storm had just started its soccer practice when Brittany Hall and her father came walking into the gymnasium. Although Mr. Hall called Kaylee's father aside, it was not too difficult for Kaylee and the others to pick up the main points of the conversation, the gymnasium's acoustics being what they were.

Brittany had missed the last two games. The general assumption had been that she had quit the team, probably embarrassed and angry over being yanked out of the game against the Clash by Coach O'Shay.

"Yeah, Brittany, was mad," Mr. Hall, a wide-shouldered man with a thick moustache, admitted to Coach O'Shay. "And to tell the truth, I wasn't real happy. But we talked it over, and Brittany's got something to say."

Brittany had been staring at the gym floor while standing next to her father, but now she looked up at Coach O'Shay. "I want to apologize," she said haltingly, but without shame. "I'm sorry I missed the games. Dad and me, we talked it over though. I'm no quitter. I . . . I want to come back and finish the season. Quitting, well, that's not the kind of person I am."

Coach O'Shay regarded her silently for a moment and then let out a long breath. "You realize that you probably won't get a lot of playing time right away. You'll have to earn your way back onto the field. And I'm not talking about talent. You'll have to show me you're willing to work hard and support your teammates."

Brittany nodded, dropping her eyes to the floor again.

"All right," said Mr. Hall, rubbing his hands together. "I'm glad we could work this out. Brittany and me, we're kind of stubborn, you know? But a commitment is a commitment. You don't leave your teammates hanging!" Then he shook hands with Coach O'Shay and left Brittany to join the workout.

As Brittany jogged into the circle where the rest of them were stretching, Kaylee felt her already floundering heart sink a little more. She knew she would have to make a decision fairly soon. She could not go to both the soccer tournament and the dance performance.

But how could she choose? She loved Irish dance. Never before had she been part of something that made her feel so perfect and strong and happy. This overwhelming truth had convinced her of what she had to do: tell her father that she would miss the soccer tournament. There was absolutely no way her heart would allow her to miss going to Madison for the big performance. Not only was it one of Trean Gaoth's showcase events of the year, it would also be her first show with the group.

Now, however, she knew that this plan would be impossible. If Brittany--the most self-absorbed, mean-spirited person that Kaylee had ever met—had swallowed her pride and returned to the soccer team, how could Kaylee bail out on them? If Kaylee left her teammates short-handed in order to go to Madison while Brittany stayed with the soccer team and played, who was really the most self-absorbed?

How would it make her father look?

She spoke to him as they rode home from the workout.

"Dad, I'm going to the tournament."

Her father glanced at her skeptically. "What about your big dance show?"

She tried to hold her voice steady. "I want to go to the soccer tournament. I want to be there for the team."

Her father's gaze bounced from the road to his daughter. Then a smile broke across his face. "That's my girl! The way you've been playing lately, I knew you wouldn't be able to resist! This is where your real talent is, sweetheart!"

Kaylee smiled, fighting to hold back the tears. "I guess so, dad."

Eighteen

The first Monday in March, Annie held a dress rehearsal for the Madison show. Kaylee still had not told her that she would miss the St. Patrick's Day performance.

"Annie will be disappointed," said Caitlin as they slipped into their school dresses. It was the first time Kaylee had worn hers outside of her house. "But she'll understand. It would be different if you were a third- or fourth-year dancer who was competing at the pre-champion level. You've only been at it a few months. Besides, there are at least ten dancers in your number. They can get through it just fine without you."

"It's still hard to tell her," said Kaylee, helping Caitlin adjust her cape. "I really love Irish dancing and I don't want to blow it."

Caitlin patted her friend's forearm. "It'll be okay," she said, sympathetically. Then a concerned look clouded her face. "Of course, Miss Helen won't be too happy."

Kaylee nodded grimly. "She'll be thinking I'm another Lizzie Martin."

Caitlin laughed. "You wish! I don't think either of us inherited that kind of talent!"

Although Kaylee wished she were going to Madison, she was glad that the dress rehearsal would at least give her a chance to see all the dancers in full costume. Trean Gaoth performed many shows in the Milwaukee area on the days leading up to St. Patrick's Day, but the annual Madison show had always been special because it was in the state capital in front of thousands. It was also televised.

Beth O'Shay had not been able to attend the dress rehearsal because of her work schedule. Kaylee's father had Monday soccer practice for the Green Storm. As a result, Mrs. Hubbard had driven the two girls to the school and now helped Kaylee get ready. Her white socks had to be pulled tight against her calves and anchored in placed with "sock glue". Caitlin helped her apply subtle touches of makeup. Mrs. Hubbard pulled back Kaylee's hair and pinned the special wig—a mass of bobbing curls that perfectly matched her own hair--in place.

All dancers had the option of purchasing a wig or of putting dozens of curlers into their hair the night before a show—a laborious project that often took hours and then made it difficult for them to sleep. The vast majority purchased a wig. Somehow, Kaylee's parents had managed this expense. She suspected it had something to do with a conversation between her parents that she had overheard.

Beth O'Shay: *Because of my work schedule, you'll probably have to put the curlers in Kaylee's hair the night before most of her shows.*

Tom O'Shay: *How many curlers?*

Beth O'Shay: *One hundred. Maybe one hundred and twenty.*

And suddenly, Kaylee had a wig.

Last of all, Kaylee slipped on her school dress. Caitlin zipped up the back, fastened her friend's cape and then stepped back. "Take a look in the mirror," instructed Caitlin. With mirrors all along the dance floor walls on one side, Kaylee did not have to go far to find one. As she stepped in front of the glass, she hardly recognized the figure staring back at her. She looked like one of the *Isle of Green Fire* dancers. She looked more beautiful than she had ever imagined she could look.

"You look great," said Caitlin, coming up behind her. "Come on! We're ready to start!"

Kaylee followed her friend to one side of the main practice floor where other girls in their group had assembled. Annie emerged from a gaggle of costumed girls still on the carpeted entry area and stepped onto the dance floor. She pivoted a half turn and addressed the group, her green eyes twinkling, a broad smile on her face.

"Tara and Miss Helen are going to line up the groups at the sides. They'll send you out when your music begins. We want to treat this just like the real show, so look sharp, point the toes, let the audience feel your energy!"

Annie stepped off the practice floor, leaving the large middle section empty. Most of the performance groups hustled into position along the walls. The show would be composed of ten separate dance numbers. Of the more than three hundred dancers who belonged to Trean Gaoth, only about two dozen practiced with Kaylee's beginner group. As a result, Kaylee noticed scores of unfamiliar faces. "Sometimes you'll see some of the other girls at feisanna or big performances," Caitlin had explained. "And if we get to be really good, we'll get moved up into different practice groups and meet new people." Caitlin also mentioned that some of the more advanced dancers were in three or four different dances. Kaylee and Caitlin would dance in only one.

Most of the girls standing ready along the sides wore their navy-and-gold Trean Gaoth school dresses. However, a good number of the older girls wore solo dresses. While she had heard Caitlin and some of the others talk about these dresses, Kaylee had never seen them before.

They were wonderful.

In a way, the solo dresses were like snowflakes—each one unique. Some dresses were green or silver or blue, but she also found vibrant purples and oranges and pinks. The entire rainbow seemed to be represented. Most of the solo dresses sparkled as if covered by gems, which was another way they differed from the school dresses. And while the girls in school dresses wore simple white knitted headbands, those with solo dresses were crowned with jewel-studded tiaras that completed the image of a royal princess.

"When do we get dresses like that?" Kaylee whispered to Caitlin.

Caitlin followed Kaylee's gaze to the girls in solo costumes. "You have to earn them by getting medals in higher-level competition. Mom says they cost three or four times the price of a school dress!"

The financial reality jolted Kaylee out of the daydream in which she saw herself in a glittering silver dress. It was a good thing, for the dancers were set to begin the exciting opening number, which combined bits and pieces of several different dances. At one point, about sixty girls would be on stage. The second number would be a hard shoe piece that everyone referred to as "St. Patrick's Day". Caitlin explained to Kaylee that many people danced this number at feises. "Girls all over the world dance the same steps that we do for St. Patrick's Day," explained Caitlin. "For almost every other dance, each school's steps are unique."

Kaylee's group would dance third.

The show began with the simple sound of accordion music floating on the air. Two lines of girls in hard shoes moved onto the performance area in perfect unison. They came together into one line, dazzled the audience with their footwork as the music built, and then split into four sets. Two more lines of girls now moved onstage behind them, their footsteps blending in seamlessly with the girls already onstage. Then, the dancers in hard shoes split down the middle and flowed like two waves to opposite corners, replaced by eight dancers in ghillies dancing in two sets. Two more sets joined them, and the sixteen dancers wove themselves around the stage, each set doing what the other was doing, yet each moving in its own orbit, carried along on the music like feathers. Before long, more hard shoe dancers appeared and the ghillies drifted off. The music seemed to build, slightly louder, more frenzied as each new group took the stage, until finally, a line of eight girls in dazzling solo costumes appeared, each offering a few unique steps of her own, then all eight joining together in a spectacular, ear-splitting, rapid-fire finale that ended so suddenly and perfectly that it was as if a lightning bolt had struck the studio. Parents applauded wildly, as did the dancers standing along the walls.

Next up was the St. Patrick's Day number, a hard shoe dance that Kaylee liked and which she hoped to learn next year. As the dancers marched onto the performance area, Tara stepped to the front and made some remarks about the previous number, remarks similar to what she would make at the actual show. She explained that the number had been designed to give the audience a preview of the many different dance styles they would see in the next hour. Then Tara stepped away and the St. Patrick's Day music began. In a minute and a half, it was over, and it was Kaylee's turn.

Kaylee's group consisted of ten girls who paraded onto the dance floor in two lines. Kaylee stood in the back row. The music for their reel began.

Knee two-three-four-five-six-seven switch point switch point pull back step in switch point two-three-four-five-six-seven leap two-three switch point hop back.

Kaylee felt as if she were flying. She always felt wonderful when dancing, but doing the routine in her school dress seemed to give her extra energy. Her toes seemed to point effortlessly, her movements became crisper, and her timing was perfect. After a few measures, the first row fell back and Kaylee's row moved to the front. Kaylee could tell she was hitting every step perfectly, and her teammates seemed to be in the zone, too. Most of the faces in the audience registered as a blur, but then she recognized Annie, right up front, nodding, a smile on her face. *She thinks we're doing a good job,* thought Kaylee, whose own smile grew just a bit broader. *Too bad mom couldn't be here to see this,* thought Kaylee. *We are so on!*

The entire dance took less than two minutes. At the end, Kaylee and the others stopped, stood straight, pointed the toes on their right feet, and gave a modest bow.

Her group filed off the dance floor and onto the carpeted area. Since it was their only number in the program, they could now join the audience. The first thing Kaylee and the other girls in her group did was exchange hugs, which led to an exchange of giggles, compliments, shrieks of joy and general silliness.

"We rocked!" said Caitlin as she hugged Kaylee for the third time.

"I can't believe how awesome we were!" agreed Kaylee.

The fourth number had begun by now—a small group of boys dressed in black pants and shirts. They were roughly Kaylee's age, give or take a few years. Kaylee guessed that girls outnumbered the boys about forty-to-one at Trean Gaoth, and Caitlin had informed her that this was pretty much the way it was at Irish dance schools everywhere. As the boys— straight as fence posts yet nimble as gymnasts— completed their routine, Kaylee's teammates began to find places to stand in order to watch the rest of the show. Kaylee looked around for a good spot that wasn't going to leave her stuck behind a six-foot-tall parent. As she scanned the crowd, she recognized someone whose presence surprised her.

Her father.

He was standing toward the back of the group, not watching the dance floor. His gaze was on his daughter. Tom O'Shay smiled when their eyes made contact, and then Kaylee weaved her way over to him. When she arrived, the two of them stepped farther behind the crowd so that they could hear each other over the music.

"What are you doing here?" asked Kaylee.

Her father looked a little hurt by this question. "I wanted to see you dance. I suppose I embarrassed you."

"No," said Kaylee. "I'm glad you came. I'm just surprised. I didn't think you were very interested in this sort of thing." Then she remembered the soccer practice. "What about the Green Storm?"

Mr. O'Shay made a no-big-deal gesture. "Jackie's dad is filling in as coach for today."

Kaylee nodded. Her father seemed to want to say something, but hesitated, lost the words. His eyes remained fixed on Kaylee, however, and she saw something in his face that seemed almost like pride. After a moment, she decided to say something to break the uncomfortable silence. "Well, that was it for me. I'm only in that one number."

Mr. O'Shay offered a little smile. "It was wonderful. I'm amazed at what your feet can do! I guess . . ." He shook his head, his voice trailing off momentarily before resuming. "I guess I never really paid much attention to your dancing before. Never thought of it as much more than girls hopping around on a stage. But it's beautiful. And I can tell it's hard work." He paused here, and his gaze narrowed on Kaylee. "And you're very good at it."

Kaylee felt herself blush a bit. She turned toward the dance floor so that her father would not notice. Two sixteen-year-old girls who competed in the champion class were now dancing, each seemingly attempting to outdo the other. She was fascinated by the height of their leaps, the speed and precision of their movements. As the dance came to a close and ecstatic applause rained down on the two dancers, Kaylee's father tapped her on the elbow.

"So is that what you'll be able to do someday?" he asked, pointing toward the dance floor.

Kaylee gave him a broad smile. A year ago she would have said, *I'll never be able to do that.* Three months ago she would have said it. Last week, perhaps. If someone had asked, she might have said it an instant before she saw her father in the crowd today. But his words had changed all of that.

"Yes!" said Kaylee confidently.

He nodded as if he had known the answer before asking the question.

They stood together watching the rest of the show. Afterwards, Annie gathered the dancers around her on the wide floor, most of them standing to avoid wrinkling their dresses. "You looked fabulous!" she said enthusiastically. "There are a few minor things we can work on in classes before the show date, but overall, it's obvious that you've worked hard. You're ready!"

Basking in the afterglow of the successful dress rehearsal, Kaylee changed out of her costume and covered it with the plastic dry cleaning bag her parents had given her for protecting it. Caitlin and most of the girls in the dance school had special navy-and-gold dress bags with "Trean Gaoth" and the school logo on the side.

Someday.

She met her father near the entrance doors and the two walked carefully across the packed snow and ice crusts that the plow had missed in the parking lot. Mr. O'Shay started the car and leaned back in his seat to let it warm up for a minute. Kaylee could tell he was thinking about something.

"Sweetheart," he said suddenly, "I want you to do your dance show."

The statement was so unexpected that at first, Kaylee did not even understand the words. "What?"

"Your St. Patrick's Day show," said her father. "I want you to go to Madison on the bus with your team." He paused and clarified this. "Your dance team."

Kaylee's heart leaped. She had been looking forward to this show for months. She had imagined herself dancing with her group, a part of something dynamic and athletic and beautiful.

"But," she asked tentatively, "what about the soccer tournament?"

Her father smiled, leaned forward and kissed her on the forehead. "You're good at soccer. You've really blossomed as a player this year. You don't know how proud of you I am for that. And I know that you like soccer. Not in the same way I do, but you like it when you score a goal or steal a pass. And

I think you like that I'm your coach."   He paused here, looking at Kaylee, it seemed, as though seeing her for the first time.   "But you love Irish dance.   It would be selfish of me to stand in the way of that."

Kaylee threw herself forward, giving her father an enormous hug.   If there had not been a door to stop him, both would have tumbled out of the car backwards and landed on the ground.

"Thank you, Daddy!"   She kissed him on the cheek, but then caught herself.   "What about the other girls on the soccer team?   What will they think when the coach's daughter doesn't play?"

Mr. O'Shay waved a hand gently, dismissively in front of her.   "Don't worry about that.   I'm your parent, and I let you join both dance and soccer.   It's my fault that you're in this situation, and it's my responsibility to deal with it."

It was as if a glorious window had opened. Kaylee felt like laughing and crying and dancing and hugging everyone she could find.   When she got home, she would practice again.   Then she would watch *Isle of Green Fire* for the jillionth time.

Nineteen

On Tuesday, Mr. O'Shay drove his daughter and Caitlin to the Cream City Mall on the western edge of Milwaukee. Going to the mall was a rare treat for Kaylee, but Mr. O'Shay knew his daughter enjoyed "window shopping" at the various stores, even though most of the merchandise was out of her price range. "My price range, basically, is anything that's free," Kaylee told her friend.

Mr. O'Shay had wanted to pick up a birthday present for his wife. "She'd probably appreciate something from the mall a bit more than a sack of washers from Rosemary Hardware," he told the girls. He also figured a trip to the mall would be a nice way to reward his daughter's hard work in dance as well as on the soccer field.

Of course Will came along, too.

"Will and I are going to the arcade," said Mr. O'Shay as they entered the gleaming, bustling mall. Every surface was white or silver, except for the colorful signs above the shops. "We'll meet you back here in an hour!"

The mall had two levels which stretched out in four directions from a wide-open central hub. The most exciting and exclusive stores were clustered around this hub, and so this was where Kaylee and Caitlin headed.

The center of the mall also featured a fountain, a waterfall, raised platforms for displays or special performances and a breathtaking skylight sixty feet above. The last time Kaylee had visited the Cream City Mall, some famous choir group from Milwaukee had been performing on one of the platforms, and the sounds of their beautiful voices had filled the mall with carols. The time before that, a Milwaukee model railroad club had set up working displays on the stages. Will had enjoyed that.

As Caitlin and Kaylee approached the hub, they heard music. Maybe another choir, thought Kaylee. Or a high school band.

As she listened, however, something seemed familiar about the music. The grainy strains of accordion filled their ears—music that both girls recognized. Then they heard the synchronized slap of hard shoe on dance floor. The girls looked at each other, their eyes bulging.

"It's Irish dancers!" squealed Caitlin.

"Did Trean Gaoth have a show scheduled for the mall today?" asked Kaylee, who knew that sometimes Annie took small groups of experienced dancers to special performances, especially around St. Patrick's Day.

Caitlin shook her head. "I don't think so."

The two broke into a jog and stopped at a large sign on an easel where the hallway opened into the wide, central area.

Come see the
Golden Academy
of Irish Dancing

"Simply the Best!"

6-7 p.m. on Tuesday

"Ah!" said Caitlin, some of her initial enthusiasm now gone. "The *Evil Empire!*"

Kaylee asked her what she meant as the two walked to the large raised platform where the dance group's footfalls echoed in perfect unison.

"They think they're better than everyone else," said Caitlin huffily. "And they kind of are. Golden Academy girls win all kinds of medals at almost every feis, and size-wise they're almost as big as Trinity," noted Caitlin, referring to the nationally-famous Chicago-based Irish dance school.

An enormous crowd watched the dancers, and so Kaylee and Caitlin climbed onto the landing of a wide stairway leading to the mall's second level.

Then they leaned against the chrome railing, where they had a perfect view of the dance area.

The crowd applauded the dance that had only just ended as the dancers bowed and then moved offstage. Different music began now, and another group of dancers in ghillies gracefully poured out from the sides. Golden Academy's school dresses, Kaylee noticed, were quite different from Trean Gaoth's. "They've got tights instead of white socks," she said to Caitlin.

Caitlin nodded, but continued to watch, mesmerized by the clockwork movements of the bodies below.

In addition to the black tights, the Golden Academy school dress was white with an intricate dark-green Celtic knot that defined the edges. On the cape, the letters GA were centered, one slightly above the other, with a gilded Celtic braid encircling them.

"They are good," said Kaylee, watching them move in time to the recorded Irish tunes blasting from nearby speakers.

"They should be," said Caitlin haughtily. "They have a thousand dancers and a huge new dance studio not far from here."

As the dance continued, Kaylee noticed several young ladies in Golden Academy school dresses moving through the crowd, handing brochures to parents and young girls. When one came near, Kaylee reached over the railing and the girl handed a brochure up to her.

"What do you want with that?" asked Caitlin, wrinkling her nose at the paper.

"Just curious," said Kaylee.

As Caitlin turned back to the dancers on the platform, Kaylee skimmed the brochure. Among other things, she learned that Caitlin had not been far off when she mentioned "a thousand dancers". The studio near the Cream City Mall in the western suburbs had actually been built seventeen years ago by Bernard Golden, owner of a chain of clothing stores, who then put his daughter, Clarissa, in charge. The school had grown from twenty-five dancers in its first year to its present size, which had required several additions along the way and a complete makeover of the building just three years ago. It was now considered "the most impressive facility for the teaching of Irish dance in the Midwest". Color photographs underscored this claim.

The brochure also listed the many achievements of the group, including several individual World titles.

"Our mission at Golden Academy, is the same as our motto," the brochure quoted Clarissa Golden. "To be 'simply the best'!"

The dancers in ghillies were now leaving the platform to waves of enthusiastic applause. As the noise died, three dancers about Kaylee's age in breathtaking solo dresses and hard shoes positioned themselves along the back of the dancing area. They stood motionless, toes pointed, smiles radiant. The music began and each dancer in turn performed a mesmerizing, pounding, visually spectacular showcasing of her talents. First came a girl with dark curls in a sparkling red dress whose leaps were higher than Kaylee had ever seen. Then a red-haired dancer in a dazzling green outfit moved with such grace that Kaylee was certain that she was watching an angel. As the girl was finishing her turn, Kaylee felt a strong hand on her shoulder. She assumed it was her father, but when she turned, she found that it belonged to another man, who wore a thin smile. His light brown hair, moustache and full face seemed familiar to Kaylee, and after a moment, she realized who he was.

"Mr. Hall!" said Kaylee, surprised to see Brittany's father.

"I thought I recognized you up here, Kaylee," he said. Then he indicated the dancers with a gesture. "They're quite something, aren't they? Some say they're one of the best dance groups in the country!"

Kaylee heard Caitlin clear her throat.

"They are good," said Kaylee, dividing her attention between Mr. Hall and the performance.

"Did your father drive you here to see them?" asked Mr. Hall, his eyes traveling around to see if Mr. O'Shay were nearby.

"He's in the arcade with my brother," said Kaylee. "We didn't know they were dancing today. When we heard the music, we stopped to watch. Caitlin and I, we're in Irish dancing."

Mr. Hall's eyebrows rose slightly. "Really? Which group?"

"Trean Gaoth!" said Caitlin proudly.

"Ah," said Mr. Hall with a slight nod. "The bowling alley group."

Kaylee was not sure what he meant by the comment, but was impressed that he seemed to have heard of Trean Gaoth. "Are you a fan of Irish dancing?" she asked Mr. Hall. "Is that why you're here?"

Now Mr. Hall smiled broadly. "I'm a fan of my daughter," he said, pointing to the dance area. "Brittany's been dancing since she was six, and she's up right now. I'm going up top to get some pictures!"

As he bounded up the remaining stairs to the mall's open second level, Kaylee's head snapped back toward the performance below. The third girl, with blonde curls and a stunning white, jeweled dress moved like lightning across the stage. Kaylee had never seen such fast feet.

Brittany Hall.

"Is she that soccer jerk you were telling about at the sleepover?" asked Caitlin, watching the performance with rapt attention.

Kaylee nodded, letting her chin slip down onto her hands.

Caitlin watched Brittany easily execute a perfect front scissors. "The soccer jerk is good."

Kaylee sighed, her breath clouding the chrome railing. "Wouldn't you know it." She would never have recognized Brittany if Mr. Hall had not pointed her out, disguised as she was by the bright curls and the makeup.

Kaylee and Caitlin visited stores for a half hour after Brittany's dance, but Kaylee's preoccupation with this new knowledge about Brittany kept her from enjoying the experience as she would have normally. They met up with Mr. O'Shay and Will at the designated time, and her father treated them to soft pretzels at a mall vendor before dropping off Caitlin in Paavo and then heading back to Rosemary.

They arrived home to find the house uncharacteristically dark.

"Mom must still be at work," said Kaylee, walking to her room where she removed her safely-stowed dress from under her bed. Dance dresses were supposed to be stored flat, according to Caitlin, not draped onto a hanger. Grandma must be at the Stitchin' Kitchen, too, she thought, as her eyes traveled over the school dress, comparing it mentally to Brittany's magnificent solo dress.

She entered the kitchen to find her father reading a note, a concerned look on his face.

"Come on," he said curtly, as he dropped the note onto the kitchen table. "We've got to drive back to Paavo."

"What's wrong," said Kaylee, suddenly afraid of the look in his eyes.

"Your grandmother," said Mr. O'Shay. "They took her to the hospital."

He called Will and the three of them grabbed their coats again as they headed out the door.

"What happened?" asked Kaylee, scrambling into her seat and clicking the buckle.

"Your mother's note doesn't say a lot," said Mr. O'Shay. "But she thinks it's Grandma's heart."

Twenty

Kaylee couldn't stop the tears. *Don't die, grandma,* she prayed as her father raced along the highway back toward Paavo. She thought of her grandmother reading to her at Christmas, of the time they had spent sewing together, of the many holidays they had spent at Grandma Birdsall's house before Grandpa Birdsall had passed away. Even Will, who was normally oblivious to everything that could not be destroyed by pushing a button on a keypad, wimpered softly in the backseat.

Kaylee also thought of the times she had avoided her grandmother, and of the times she had said things that she now regretted. This made the tears come even harder.

"I should have a cell phone," said Mr. O'Shay. "Your mother could have called me right away."

The drive seemed to take forever. Finally they crested the hill and veered into the wide parking lot in front of Paavo Community Hospital. Kaylee and Will held their father's hands as they moved briskly through the double doors and approached the information desk. The volunteer on duty directed them to the emergency unit, and they headed off down a beige hallway.

Ominous signs bearing the red word EMERGENCY told them when they had arrived. A woman in front of two closed doors listened to their questions and then issued them visitor badges. "Room ten," she said, and touched a button that started a buzzing sound near the double doors. One of them opened, and the children followed their father inside.

A large, oval-shaped countertop dominated the center of the room. Inside of this oval were people in white or blue coats, some sitting at computer workstations, others jotting information onto forms attached to clipboards, others standing and talking to people across the countertop. A tile area perhaps ten feet wide surrounded the oval, and at the edge of this were the patient cubicles. Kaylee's father spotted the cubicle marked "ten" and headed for it.

She's dead, Kaylee said to herself as they neared the cubicle. Somehow she had known this as soon as her father had revealed the contents of the note on the kitchen table. She did not want to see her grandmother that way. Would her eyes be open, staring, accusing? Or would she be covered with a sheet? She braced herself. *I'm sorry, grandma. I'm sorry I wasn't nicer to you. I was selfish, and now it's too late.*

143 / Rod Vick

The door to the cubicle stood half open, but a curtain had been pulled across the opening inside. Kaylee's father paused, raised his fist, uncertain whether to knock. Then he lowered his hand, pulled open the curtain and walked in.

"Oh Tom," Kaylee heard her mother exclaim, and Beth O'Shay threw her arms around her husband and held him, shaking. Kaylee stepped around the two of them, not really wanting to see, but knowing at the same time that she had to see.

Her grandmother lay on an emergency room gurney with wheels and adjustable tubular metal side rails to keep the patient from falling out. A blanket covered her to the midsection, and the bed had been adjusted so that she was almost in a sitting position. An IV bag hung at the left side of the bed, and various monitors clicked and blinked nearby.

Other than that, her grandmother—who surveyed their arrival with a pleasant smile--looked just fine.

"My goodness, Kaylee, you look awful!" said Grandma Birdsall with a look of sudden concern. "Come here, precious." Her grandmother held out her arms, both of which had either wires or tubes attached to them.

Kaylee moved forward, wiping the tears from her face—which was a waste of effort, for they were replaced with fresh saltwater immediately—and gave her grandmother a hug, being careful not to dislodge any of the medical equipment.

"I thought . . . I thought . . ." Kaylee lifted her head for a moment, then let it sink back onto her grandmother's shoulder. She also gathered Will in as he now came close.

"I'm fine, Kaylee," said the old woman, smoothing her granddaughter's hair. She kissed her grandson's forehead. "I'm a tough old girl, Will."

Hearing this, Kaylee's father looked to his wife.

"They're still doing tests," said Beth O'Shay. "Nothing has been ruled out. She didn't have any chest pain. No shortness of breath. She just passed out."

"I've had a little cold," said Grandma Birdsall. "It's probably just a virus that's got my system messed up."

Beth O'Shay nodded. "We'll let the doctors sort it out, Mom."

Suddenly Grandma Birdsall seemed to remember something and smiled at Kaylee and Will. "So how was your trip to the mall?"

*

They sat in the emergency unit for hours. Since Grandma Birdsall did not seem to be suffering in any way (other than the occasional observation that she would prefer to be in her own bed, which was much more comfortable), the doctor handling her case opted to check her in to a regular hospital room rather than keep her in the intensive care unit.

The initial tests did not seem to indicate a heart attack.

"Tomorrow we're going to do a stress test," said the doctor. "That will tell us more about how her heart is functioning and whether we need to schedule other procedures."

Beth O'Shay decided to stay overnight in the hospital with her mother. The chair next to Grandma Birdsall's bed was actually a comfortable recliner and there were blankets in the dresser next to the bed. Kaylee, her brother and their father arrived home just a few minutes before midnight.

"I think we'll let you sleep in a little later than usual," said Mr. O'Shay. "I'll call the school in the morning and explain the situation."

Thank you, Dad, thought Kaylee as she drifted off to sleep, exhausted.

*

Kaylee woke at about nine in the morning. She shuffled groggily to the living room, still wearing the clothes she had worn the previous day. Will was already up playing video games. *Probably destroying alien life forms since sunrise*, thought Kaylee.

On the kitchen table, Kaylee found a note from her father.

Talked to your mom this morning. Grandma had a good night. More tests today. Both send their love. I'll be home at noon to take you kids to school. Be ready. Can't afford to be late getting back to work or they'll take it out of my pay. Love, Dad.

Kaylee smiled. Grandma was doing all right so far. She and Will had a few hours to relax before they would head back to school. But they had to be ready on time, or Dad would be in trouble.

They'll take it out of my pay. That's what her father had written. Money was always tight at the O'Shay house, yet they always found money for her dance lessons, and for soccer for both Will and Kaylee. But how? Kaylee knew of the Stitchin' Kitchen's money problems. And her father drove a ten-year-old car and shopped at the secondhand store. There couldn't be money for dance and soccer, yet there always was.

And there had been money for her dance dress.

A gorgeous dress. A dress from her dreams that they could not possibly afford.

Grandma Birdsall helped Kaylee's mother pay the bills at the Stitchin' Kitchen when Beth O'Shay had a slow month. Was her grandmother helping in other ways, too?

That had to be it. Kaylee felt a lump in her throat. When she had started dancing, her sewing time with her grandmother had come to an end. Yet, Grandma Birdsall had paid for her dance lessons even though they had taken Kaylee away from her.

And the dress . . .

Kaylee walked purposefully back through the living room to her bedroom. She carefully retrieved the plastic-covered costume which she had placed beneath her bed just before falling asleep the night before. Removing the covering, she lay the dress out flat on her bed, all navy and gold with wonderful Celtic embroidery complementing the elegant Trean Gaoth logo. She ran her hand lightly over the heavy material. Even now, two and a half months after receiving the dress as a Christmas gift, Kaylee felt a thrill every time she looked at it. The first time she had worn it, the dress had seemed like more than a simple article of clothing, more than a uniform. It had seemed like a part of her.

Kaylee lifted up the hem of the dress, searching. It took her only a moment. Tiny letters had been hand-stitched into the underside of the hem: KB.

Now she knew why the dress had always felt like a part of her.

Twenty-One

"Let's go, Kaylee!" Tom O'Shay called across the living room, checking his watch. His daughter was in Grandma Birdsall's room. Who knew what they were working on?

Grandma Birdsall had come home after three days of tests. The doctors put her on five different pills. Expensive pills, according to Kaylee's father. Awful tasting pills, according to Grandma Birdsall.

Beth O'Shay had spent a lot of time at the hospital, which meant the income from the Stitchin' Kitchen would probably be down again this month.

With less than a week before the big soccer tournament, Kaylee's father seemed constantly on edge. He consulted his watch again. Although he had more than enough time, he had to drop Kaylee off at Trean Gaoth Academy on the way, and he wanted to be at soccer practice early. Today was the last Monday soccer practice, and there was so much he wanted to go over with the girls.

"Kaylee!" he called again.

Kaylee emerged from the bedroom, waving back at her grandmother who was hidden from where Tom stood.

"Love you!" said Kaylee, smiling. "We can work more on the border tomorrow!"

Mr. O'Shay immediately noticed that something wasn't right.

"We're going to be late!" he said, frustrated. "Hurry and change into your dance clothes!"

She was wearing a t-shirt, soccer shorts and her shin guards.

"I'm ready," said Kaylee brightly. "Just let me grab my coat."

Her father stood there, trying to process the image. "But," he said hesitantly, "you've got dance practice."

"No," Kaylee shook her head. "Soccer."

Mr. O'Shay sighed. "Kaylee, what's going on? It's Monday. Your big show is this Saturday."

"The St. Patrick's Day show *is* this Saturday," acknowledged Kaylee, "but I've decided to do the soccer tournament instead."

Her father blinked uncertainly a few times. "But you love dance. And you're good at it." Now his face grew more serious. "And I already told you that it's okay if you do the dance show."

"I know," said Kaylee. And she did. She knew that her father was willing to make the sacrifice. She knew that a lot of people were making sacrifices. Her mother had sacrificed the success of her business in order to spend time at the hospital with Grandma Birdsall. Grandma Birdsall had sacrificed her time and money to make Kaylee's dress and to pay for her dance lessons. She had even sacrificed her own feelings.

Now it was Kaylee's turn to sacrifice.

Mr. O'Shay stood back assessing his daughter for a moment. Then he gave her a hug and the two of them headed out to the car.

Though Miss Helen would grumble, Kaylee knew that Annie would understand her decision. The dance number would go on without her. There would be other dance shows. Next year, there would be feisanna, too. That chapter of Kaylee's life was just beginning, and she felt excited just thinking about the possibility of dancing in competition, of perhaps one day being as good as the two girls that she and her father had watched at the dress rehearsal.

Kaylee also understood that the soccer chapter of her life was drawing to a close, and this brought a deep sadness. Her father loved soccer. He had always wanted Kaylee to be a great player. Now, however, he understood that Kaylee had to choose her own road.

This weekend, she would make her father proud. She would give it everything she had.

And her heart would be dancing.

Two roads diverged in a wood, and I—
I took the one less traveled by
And that has made all the difference.

RF

Kaylee O'Shay, Irish Dancer
Book Two: GREEN STORM

Big changes are in store for Kaylee O'Shay in her second year of Irish dancing. Now she and Caitlin are learning hard shoe dances and preparing for the excitement of their first feis.

But not everything in Kaylee's life is going smoothly. As Irish dance consumes more of Kaylee's time, her relationships with her father and with her best friend, Jackie, are strained to the breaking point. Because of Brittany Hall, Kaylee gets in trouble at school. Worst of all, a tragic accident threatens to destroy her dancing dreams.

For more information about the Kaylee O'Shay series, including *Kaylee's Choice, Green Storm* and the rest of the books in Kaylee's incredible journey, visit the official online site at www.kayleeoshay.com.

If you are enjoying the Kaylee O'Shay, Irish Dancer series by Rod Vick, check out *The Irish Witch's Dress* and its sequel, *The Irish Witch's Tiara*. On the following pages, you can catch a sneak peek at the first chapter of The Irish Witch's Dress, a tale of an enchanted dress, a vengeful Celtic sorceress, a gem-studded tiara, and a young girl who wants to be a cham;pion!

The Irish Witch's Dress

1

"We must keep our voices very low, lest they hear us," said John O'Malley to his eleven-year-old daughter. The two of them sat on the edge of her bed in the dark loft of the farm house. Had someone approached them from behind, the pair would have appeared to be staring at nothing at all, for their faces hovered inches from the painted wall boards. However, their eyes were actually fixed on a thin opening where a plank had shrunk, creating a viewing sliver that overlooked the kitchen and dining areas below.

"I don't see anything," whispered Katie.

"There's nothing to see—yet," said her father. "If they come, you'll know it. They usually arrive around midnight."

Katie knew the time must be close. She had gone to bed two hours ago, as had her mother, who slept in the large bedroom downstairs. Her father had come up and awakened her—as he had promised—just a few minutes ago. Katie still felt heavy with sleep, but excited, too. She had never seen *them* before, had always thought them the creation of adult storytellers bent on frightening or disciplining children.

A part of her wondered whether this was her father's mission as well. He had already told her they did not come every night, which provided a ready excuse if midnight arrived without the creatures. Yet, it was not like her father to spin yarns as a means of encouraging her cooperation.

But still…could something so fantastic be true? A shiver shook her. Although she wore a cotton nightgown that hung from her auburn curls to her toes, she now pulled the quilt from the bed around her shoulders as well.

"You're shaking," observed her father, speaking just loudly enough for her ears to hear. "Are you frightened?"

"Just cold," she whispered, although this was only partially true.

"You don't have anything to worry about, you know," he said. "The stone is ready. There won't be any mischief."

Although she could not see it in the dark, Katie had watched her father drizzle honey into a hole in the center of a flat stone that now sat on a bench in front of the hearth. A gift for the visitors. He had also left a bowl of milk.

Yet, as the minutes ticked by and she became more fully awake, Katie began to have second thoughts about their adventure. It frightened her to think that there might be a world of extraordinary beings that, under certain conditions, intersected with her own world. It occurred to Katie that if she crawled back into bed right now and succeeded in falling asleep, she could continue to pretend the creatures did not exist. Once she saw them, however, she would always have the knowledge that, on some nights, they were right there in her house while she and her parents slept.

Another shudder.

Katie was about to say *Maybe they're not coming* and had begun to inch her way back onto the center of the mattress, when she detected a slight movement in the darkness of the kitchen, something so subtle that she would have easily missed it had her eyes not been straining into the moonlight-tinged darkness for the past quarter-hour. Then she detected another movement and a soft sliding sound as a window opened. A dozen small bodies scrambled almost noiselessly across the sill, one bearing a glass lamp within which burned a candle. This bathed the room in a subtle, golden glow and offered a better look at the visitors. Katie bit down on a corner of the quilt to prevent herself from accidentally crying out.

The visitors had two arms and two legs, like humans, but were roughly one-third the size of a man, with skin the color of the full moon. Their eyes were large and dark with almost no whites showing, their fingers slender and nimble. They moved with the swiftness and grace of children, though their limbs were sinewy like working men, and their faces appeared ancient and vaguely sad. Katie noticed that all were bald and also bereft of facial hair. Their neat clothing appeared to have been deftly woven from the grasses, ferns and leaves of the surrounding countryside. The mob rushed to the milk bowl and honey stone, lapping from them like starving animals.

Katie moved her lips against her father's ear. "What are they?"

Her father turned his nose into her hair and spoke, almost inaudibly. "Fairies."

Katie's eyes widened. "I thought fairies had wings and were beautiful."

Mr. O'Malley smiled. "Legends say there are many different kinds of fairies. During the day, these fairies live in the streams and meadows. It's only at night that they come into people's houses."

She watched as the fairies finished with the bowl and the stone. Then one of them spoke in a low tone, difficult to hear, yet Katie felt certain it was an unfamiliar tongue. In response, half a dozen began to sweep the floor, pull down cobwebs, scrub the coffee pot, shovel ash from the fireplace. One even sat at Mr. O'Malley's desk, donned a pair of small, wire spectacles, and began paging through Mr. O'Malley's farm records, adding figures here, jotting notes there. The rest of the fairies scrambled out the window. Katie looked to her father in question.

"They're off to milk the cows, collect the eggs, make repairs. They're workers, all of them. They do it in exchange for the milk and honey."

Katie nodded but then asked, "What if you forget to put out the milk and honey?"

"Oh, then they get upset! They pull pranks. Maybe break a china cup. Hide a favorite book. Put a dead mouse in your shoe so that you find it when you go to slip it on in the morning."

Katie cringed.

"Why do they do it?" she asked. "All the work, I mean."

Her father watched them for a moment before speaking. "I think this race of fairies may owe some sort of debt to men. Probably the result of an ancient war. And I suspect they're not entirely happy about having to pay it. I'll wager that's why they misbehave whenever they are given an excuse."

Katie said nothing. Merely watching the small creatures efficiently clean the house was fascinating.

"But there's something else," her father continued. "I believe the fairies have helped *us* a bit more than they do most people. You see, one night this past spring, howling dogs woke me. Then I heard growling and some commotion out behind the sheds. Grabbed my gun, and when I came around the corner of the byre, there was one of the beasts, baring his teeth at me and struggling with something. Thought he had a chicken, so I shot him. When I came over to take a closer look, I saw it wasn't a chicken at all, but rather one of our little fairies lying on the ground, covered in teeth marks."

Katie let out a sympathetic sigh, and her father had to shush her. She knew packs of wild dogs were rare, but, according to her father, could be dangerous even to humans.

"First time I'd ever seen a fairy, and I had to slap myself in the cheeks a time or two to make sure I wasn't dreaming. I discovered that the little soul was alive, but barely. And unconscious. I carried him back to our house, placed him on a folded up blanket near the fireplace, cleaned his wounds as well as I could. While most of his injuries were bites, there was one rip in his leafy tunic that revealed a very narrow bruise. The leg beneath it appeared to be broken. Not a typical bite injury. I went to the sink to put water in the kettle for some tea for the little fellow, and that was where I noticed a scrap of leafy fabric caught on a nail sticking up from the windowsill. It matched the fabric of the fairy's smock. The unfortunate creature had caught himself on that nail while exiting, and the window had fallen onto his leg, breaking it. That was why he had been caught by the dogs. Usually the fairies are far too quick to be caught. His shattered leg had slowed him down. Naturally I felt awful. If I had fixed that nail earlier, the dog never would have caught him. But that was neither here nor there. I finished bandaging him up, splinted his leg, set some tea and warm broth near him, and tried to get a bit of sleep. When I woke at dawn, he was gone. I fixed the nail, of course. Since then, the fairies seem to have treated us exceptionally well. I suppose they figure I saved the little fellow's life. Or tried to."

He paused here and squinted through the space between the boards, wearing the subtle smile of a man who, despite evidence staring him in the face, still could not believe he had fairies frequently paying visits to his kitchen. Then he leaned back toward his daughter.

"I wanted you to see them because I figured it's time you know. They help keep the farm running, Katie. If anything ever happens to me, you must remember to put out the milk and honey."

"Nothing's going to happen to you," hissed Katie. "So you'll have to keep remembering yourself!"

"Oh, I don't intend to forget," her father continued. "Since your mother got sick, she hasn't been able to help out as much, you know. And her medicines are pretty expensive, so I had to let go the three fellows who had worked here since your grandfather passed, God rest his soul. There's a lot of land and cattle. Without the fairies to help tend to it all, I'd probably have to sell."

This raised another question. "Is the medicine helping?"

Mr. O'Malley smiled kindly. "Do you know what really helps your mother? It's when you dance for her! Oh, how her eyes light up! You're so good and light on your feet and it's almost like she forgets the pain for just a—"

At this point Mr. O'Malley stopped talking, for he realized that, in his enthusiasm, his voice had risen above the level of a whisper. The two squinted through the crack in the wall, but the kitchen was now dark again and as silent as the heart of a stone.

"Will they come back?" asked Katie. "I mean, now that they know we've seen them?"

Mr. O'Malley squeezed her tiny shoulders and tucked her under her blankets.

"I don't know, sweetheart. I don't know."

Acknowledgements

Thanks to My Lovely Wife Marsha, a great comfort, a reliable proofreader, and a former dancer. Sweetheart, I can only assume that our daughter's dance talents can be attributed to your college involvement as a member of the University of Wisconsin—Stevens Point International Folk Dancers.

Thanks to my daughter, Haley Marie, whose own passion for Irish dance inspired me to write about it. Thank you also for reading the early draft and helping to make suggestions. You're the expert when it comes to Irish dance, sweetheart.

Thanks to Bridget Smith Jaskulski, founder and owner of Glencastle Irish Dancers of Milwaukee, Wisconsin for your help with the rough manuscript. Thank you for helping me to get the details right and accurately represent this incredible, rapidly blossoming phenomenon to the world.

Thanks to Sean Beglan, TCRG, who was the principal male lead of *Riverdance*, and who assisted with the first edition of this book.

Thank you to Mr. Merle Frimark, North American Press Representative for *Riverdance* for permission to use Mr. Sean Beglan and the *Riverdance* name in association with this book.

Thanks to Mr. Al Young, the best English teacher I ever had. No one played a greater role in motivating me to write.

Thank you to everyone who helped in ways big and small. Even if you were not named here, please know that I am enormously grateful for your contributions.

About the Author

Rod Vick has written for newspapers and magazines, has worked as an editor and has taught writing workshops and classes over the span of thirty-seven years. His short stories have appeared in a variety of literary magazines and have won both regional and national awards.   Mr. Vick was also the 2000 Wisconsin Teacher of the Year.

Rod Vick lives in Mukwonago, Wisconsin with his wife, Marsha, and children Haley and Joshua.   An occasional speaker at conferences and orientation events, he also runs marathons, enthusiastically supports his children's dance, music and soccer passions, and pitches a pretty mean horseshoe.

Other Books by Rod Vick

Green Storm

Fire & Metal

Christmas in Ireland

The Secret Ceili

The Winds of Ireland

Isle of Green Fire

Dancer in the Painted Mask

Dance of Time

The Irish Witch's Dress

The Irish Witch's Tiara

Dance of the Third-string Quarterback

www.kayleeoshay.com

Made in the USA
Middletown, DE
25 February 2020

85331281R00106